ASPECTS OF A PSYCHOPATH

ASPECTS OF A PSYCHOPATH
Alistair Langston

First published in England in 2003 by
Telos Publishing Ltd
61 Elgar Avenue, Tolworth, Surrey, KT5 9JP, England

www.telos.co.uk

ISBN: 1-903889-63-4 (paperback)
Aspects of a Psychopath © 2003 Alistair Langston.

The moral rights of the author have been asserted.

Printed in India

1 2 3 4 5 6 7 8 9 10 11 12 13 14 15

British Library Cataloguing in Publication Data.
A catalogue record for this book is available from the British Library.

To Mum and Dad,
Stephen and Christopher;
this one is for you
with thanks.

'Whoever is meant to be captured
will be captured;
Whoever is meant to be killed by the sword
will surely be killed by the sword.'

Revelation 13 vs 10.

Monday 1st January

I start the year with a pounding in my skull and the lingering taste of alcohol on my tongue. Lena, the Swedish exchange student I picked up in Bonaparte's last night, is lying bound, naked and bloody on the floor before me. She is in a placid, euphoric state, the result of a large quantity of smack that I injected into her veins prior to performing the delicate task of peeling the lightly tanned flesh from her over-ripe breasts.

Made a list of my resolutions for the next twelve months, and then scrapped it. Last year I resolved never to drink again. That idea fell by the wayside within twelve hours. As for the one I made about finding someplace better to live; I'm still here; in a shitty, one room apartment that should have been condemned years ago. I therefore see little point in making another list of promises to myself that I'm unlikely to keep. However I have decided that, having received for Christmas a leather bound diary with my name – Saul Roberts – embossed in gold lettering on the front cover, I will try to keep a written account of my daily activities. Maybe, in years to come, I can look back on these times with fond memories. That's about the nearest I'm going to get to a resolution.

8 pm Bitch! Alison telephoned to wish me a Happy New Year before letting me know that she won't be back in London until the end of the week. In the meantime, I've decided to lock Lena in the hall closet until I have thought of what I'm going to do with her!

Tuesday 2nd January

Tired. Lena kept me awake most of the night with her screams of hysteria. Fortunately, the neighbours to one side of my apartment moved out a couple of weeks ago. That was two days after I doused their front door in petrol and ignited a match, because the fat slag had sent her husband, for the umpteenth time, to tell me to turn down the volume on my television. The old bat that lives on the other side is stone deaf, and rarely ventures out of her door for fear of being attacked by youths from one or other of the gangs that regularly terrorise the residents of our estate. She keeps herself to herself and has no friends or relatives to keep an eye on her, as far as I'm aware.

At one point Lena's screams became unbearable and I contemplated the suffocation of my house guest with a plastic bag over the head, but it didn't help to discover that the only one I could find – one of the cheap ones you get from the supermarket – had a bloody big hole in it. In the end, a heavy punch in the face was all that was required to permit me a couple of hours of uninterrupted sleep.

Obviously this isn't the type of behaviour I expect from my guests. Lena is going to have to learn the hard way that I am in control of the situation. Something one would have thought she might have already grasped since Sunday night, when she led me on most of the evening; allowing me to buy her drinks and then having the gall to tell me to fuck off with that husky, Swedish tone. No-one speaks to me like that; especially not some self-centred, know it all, Scandinavian student who thinks that she has the right to pick and choose whichever man she sees fit. I'll teach her. By the time I've finished, she will be wishing she had never crossed me.

Wednesday 3rd January

Went to the newsagents and picked up a couple of papers while the shop assistant behind the counter had her back to me. Returning to the grey monolithic building in which I've lived for the past three years, I was annoyed to discover that the lift was out of order for the third time in as many weeks, having stopped somewhere between the seventh and eighth floors. By the time I'd climbed the stairs to the tenth floor and my apartment, I was exhausted.

Indoors, with a large neat vodka in hand, I settled down in the armchair and scoured the newspapers for any mention of Lena's disappearance. There was none.

Thursday 4th January

Didn't get up until twelve-thirty and then had a shower.

After something to eat I phoned Andrew, a long time drinking acquaintance, part-time dealer and occasional pimp. He knows, through bitter experience, not to ask questions about the gear I order from him, even though he is aware that I don't use it myself.

It's six-thirty in the evening, it's cold and, as usual, the central heating system isn't working. I considered going for a jog in the park earlier this afternoon, but looking out of the window at the dark, ominous clouds, and with the lifts still out of order, I decided against it.

Andrew phoned and asked if I fancied going out for a drink. Unfortunately I had to turn him down. Prior to his call I had been busy extracting Lena's teeth with a pair of pliers. I couldn't very well leave her without completing the task. It wouldn't have been fair. Besides, I couldn't leave her bleeding all over my carpet; it would take ages to clean. In the end, I suggested that we got together sometime next week.

Friday 5th January

Alison phoned again, declaring her love for me and how much she missed me. Words I could barely take seriously when, moments later, she announced that she now won't be back for another week. She then attempted to explain something about her ex taking an overdose and her own feelings of responsibility. Who the hell does she think I am? If she wants to play that game she can go ahead, but she's got another thought coming if she thinks she can pull the wool over my eyes. No-one spends a week with an ex just because he's tried to top himself. I wish the stupid fool had succeeded; maybe next time he should give me a call first and I'll make sure he does the job properly. Alison must think that by telling me, it makes everything okay. Well screw her! She may have a short memory but, unless she was lying at the time, she once said: 'It was a relationship I'd rather forget. Admittedly, I was flattered by the interest and intrigued, but I soon found out it was like dating Jekyll and Hyde. I've regretted it ever since.' Obviously she didn't regret it enough!

Saturday 6th January

Went down the pub for a quiet drink this evening and realised that I may have been a little hasty in yesterday's remarks about Alison. I actually think I miss her elfish presence; her auburn, shoulder length hair; her hazel eyes; and, more importantly, her large, firm breasts – which, as it happens, are her best assets, and far better than the pair now remaining on the Swedish bitch. The Dog and Duck isn't the same without Alison serving behind the Victorian-themed bar. She is the best looking barmaid currently employed there; which isn't saying much when you consider the competition: an elderly spinster who gave up men for horses years ago and another girl who, with a face like a wet weekend, can't even pull a pint let alone some unfortunate bugger that would have to be both blind and drunk to go with her. Of course, when she's working, the main advantage of dating Alison is that I don't have to pay the outrageous bar prices that I was charged tonight for a couple of bottles of beer!

On the way home I dropped in to Andrew's, where I took receipt of five small sachets of certain prohibited substances. Once in the apartment I hid my purchase in the toilet cistern where I keep the syringe and spare needles.

Tuesday 9th January

I can hear Lena sobbing.

When I left her a few minutes ago she was still bleeding. It was her own fault. If she had kept still while I glided the knife up between her legs, she would be in far less pain than she is now.

Wednesday 10th January

Signed on today. As usual I had to stand in a queue for half an hour within the benefits office waiting to make my mark. One day a happy, smiling face will greet me, but I won't hold my breath with anticipation. I really should start looking for a job. I'm finding it difficult without a regular income. I suppose if I hadn't lost my temper with the foreman on that building site where I worked last September, I might still be employed now. The last I heard he is still in a coma and the outlook is bleak. Fortunately. Otherwise the police would be more than interested to hear what actually happened that day. By good luck more than anything, there was no-one else around at the time.

Lena's rather quiet. She just glared at me when I went in to check on her earlier. She's up to something. I'm sure of it.

This afternoon I felt like doing nothing so, after popping down to the video shop, I put my feet up in front of the television and spent the afternoon watching Alfred Hitchcock's *Vertigo*. It's a great film.

Friday 12th January

Lena attempted to escape this morning. I was taking her some breakfast and had just untied her hands when she kicked out, sending me crashing to the floor. Within seconds she was on me, clawing at my eyes and screaming obscenities in her native tongue. A knee in her groin was enough to bring her under control, although the resounding crack was probably an indication that I had broken her pubic bone. I rebound her hands more tightly than before, then picked up the broken bowl. If she wants to eat, she can lap the cereal up like a dog.

Arrived at the station with plenty of time to spare, only to discover that Alison's train had been delayed by forty minutes. When she eventually arrived, at ten past eight, it took us another twenty minutes before we found a taxi and loaded it with her luggage. Once we reached her bedsit it didn't take me long to discover that her breasts are still as firm as ever, though as she lay silently in bed beside me I couldn't help wondering if there was something on her mind.

Saturday 13th January

Lena is becoming difficult. On opening the closet door, I was greeted by a barrage of Scandinavian abuse before my guest released her bladder and began laughing hysterically. Decided it might be wise to gag her now that Alison is around; can't have her mouthing off and giving her presence away.

Monday 15th January

Alison's made an appointment with her doctor for tomorrow. She wouldn't tell me why she was going, other than that she had been feeling under the weather the past week or so.

Wednesday 17th January

Phoned Alison to see how her visit to the doctor went; she wasn't very communicative.

Thursday 18th January

My birthday today. Twenty-six - although, with my black hair suffering from premature greyness and in desperate need of a cut, and my chin exhibiting a thick growth of stubble from not having been shaved since Tuesday, one might think otherwise.

Withdrawing out the last of my savings, I went into the West End this morning and treated myself to a new leather jacket that had been knocked down in the January sales. Alison came over after work. During a Chinese from the take-away in the High Street, she gave me a plastic watchcase. Inside there was a Seiko chronograph wristwatch – the sort of thing more suited to James Bond, with all its dials and buttons. On the back was the inscription *To Saul – With Love – Alison*. Far too sentimental for my liking.

When Alison was asleep in bed I checked the closet to see how Lena was and to take her some food. Removing her gag, I was annoyed when she spat in my face. I barely restrained myself in time from ramming my fist down her throat. Instead I picked up the carton containing the remains of the take-away, removed my erection from within my boxer shorts and jerked off over the food. Lena stared at me uncertainly but realised her earlier error when I forced open her mouth and tipped the contents of the carton down her throat. I clamped my hand over her mouth and waited until she'd swallowed the food. Going by her tears, I assume that Lena doesn't enjoy a Chinese as much as Alison and I do. Tough shit!

Friday 19th January

Managed a hundred and forty sit-ups, then showered before cashing my giro down the post office.

Alison asked me if I had ever considered the prospect of being a father. I told her to fuck off until she had something sensible to say. Now, in hindsight, I'm wondering why she should even broach the subject. For her own sake, she'd better forget the idea.

Lost my patience with Lena. Coming in late, after walking Alison back to her place, I was greeted by a frantic thumping sound from within the closet. Closer investigation revealed Lena attempting to kick her way out. Untying her limbs, I forced her to stand upright in a spread-eagle fashion before nailing her hands and feet to the sides of the closet. Her screams were still audible through the cloth of her gag. When I finished, I had to strip out of my blood-splattered clothes and take my second shower of the day.

Saturday 20th January

Spent an hour on the phone to the Samaritans describing in great detail the fun I've been having with Lena, as well as a lot more I still have planned. By the time I'd promised to strangle Lena with her own intestines I guess they'd had enough of me. They hung up with a severe reprimand for wasting their time. Idiots!

Sunday 21st January

Alison wanted to come over again tonight but I think it's pushing it too far. If Lena realises that there's someone else in the apartment then it won't be long before she finds a way of attracting their attention.

Tuesday 23rd January

Had to wrap up warm today; the flat was like a refrigerator. Lena, for reasons best known to herself, has become silent and withdrawn. Any further horrors I inflict upon her will be wasted. This has put me in a foul mood. I even shouted at the postman for making too much noise putting the letters through the door, but then what can he expect if he only ever brings me bills and final demands.

Alison's got the night off. She's invited me over to her place for a meal. Apparently there is something she wants to tell me. I hope it's not what I'm thinking. I suppose I'd better take a bottle of wine with me.

Wednesday 24th January

What a complete waste of time!

I reached Alison's at seven, only to be informed that I was too early. By the time she eventually served up the cremated chops of lamb, some ninety minutes later, we'd shared no more than a dozen or so words in conversation.

By ten, having polished off the entire bottle of Rioja that I'd taken, I made my excuses and left, lacking the revelation that I'd gone to hear.

Back at home I took my frustration out on Lena.

Thursday 25th January

Decided enough is enough. It's obvious what Alison is going to say, and I'm not going to be forced into a corner; not by anyone. If she wants to have children she can do so on her own; either that or go back to her ex, whose child it probably is anyway. Incidentally, if that is the case, then there is a situation that will have to be well and truly resolved. Intent on talking to Alison I went down the pub, but she wasn't there. Instead I found Andrew with some brunette in one of the alcoves that lined the wall opposite the bar. On seeing me, Andrew waved me over to his table and introduced his other half, Sarah.

Without being impolite, I'd hazard a guess that she is in her early thirties, making her a few years older than Andrew and me. In her youth she was probably quite good looking, although she isn't wearing so well now. Although not the most beautiful of women, she is pleasant enough and, judging by the needle marks on both arms, I would say she is probably well suited to Andrew. I'd still consider giving her one.

We sat and chatted for a while before Andrew declared it was time for the pair of them to leave and we made our farewells; Andrew helped Sarah into her coat before slipping his arm around her moderate waist and escorting her to the door.

Friday 26th January

A dreary wet day.

Awoke at 8 am to a rasping noise coming from the closet. On opening the door, I found Lena unconscious with head lolled back. She had swallowed her tongue. Not one to let her off that easily, I put my fingers down her throat and cleared her airway – certainly not the most pleasant of tasks when the individual then proceeds to vomit over you. I threw a couple of glasses of water in her face to aid her revival and allowed her time to recover before retrieving the staple gun from my toolbox.

Considered phoning Alison, but thought better of it. I've already made up my mind on the matter, and if she wants to get hold of me she knows where she can find me.

Saturday 27ᵗʰ January

My giro didn't arrive in the post today, which means I have no money to go out for a drink.

11.40 pm Desperate to get out and quench my thirst, I left the apartment at nine-thirty and made my way to the bus stop situated in front of the bakery. From there I had an ideal view of the cash dispenser located in the wall of the bank opposite. It wasn't long before a man, well into retirement, hunched over the machine, took out his wallet, inserted his cash card and entered the four-digit code. In the shadows I counted silently to five, checked that the street was clear and crept from my hiding place. Unfortunately the reaction I received from my intended victim, as I grabbed his shoulder, was not what I had anticipated. He spun around, brandishing a knife in my face. He didn't need to say anything. The message was clear enough. He was going to fight back.

What happened next, I'm not quite sure. With the adrenalin pumping through my veins and youth on my side, I wrestled the blade from the old man's grasp and, without giving him a chance, brought it down on him, slicing off three of the fingers from his raised hand. To say that I was shocked would be an understatement. I was damn well mortified to discover this stupid old codger carrying a knife that sharp. Fortunately, I refrained from revealing my surprise to him and, while he grovelled at my feet clutching his wounded hand, I gripped him beneath the chin and raised his head until he was looking directly at me. As I glared down at his pitiful figure, the colour seemed to fade from the old man's face. Perhaps it was the realisation of what was to follow; or maybe, and more likely, he detected a hint of something more as I held the lethal blade, glistening in the moonlight, above his upturned head. Whatever the reason for his pallor, one thing I can be certain of was that the last thing he saw was his own terrified image reflected in my eyes before I gouged out the orbs from the sockets of his skull.

To calm my nerves, I went over to Bonaparte's and downed several large vodkas. The fifty quid I'd lifted from my victim was hardly worth the hassle. On my way back to the flat I had to keep to the unlit alleys and cut across a couple of gardens to avoid the prying eyes of the law.

Sunday 28ᵗʰ January

Couldn't flush the toilet this morning. The pipes have frozen. I considered going out for a drink, but to make matters worse the police are crawling around all over the place. They were carrying out door-to-door enquiries earlier in their search for 'last night's assailant of a pensioner,' as one pimple faced youth, barely old enough to have finished school let alone be in the police force, bluntly put it. Unfortunately, there was nothing I wanted to add to what the youth was willing to tell me, and he went on his way.

Alison phoned, apologising for the other night. As if I care anymore.

4.45 pm The pipes have finally thawed and I can flush the toilet again.

Monday 29th January

My giro arrived in the post amongst the usual collection of bills, junk mail and circulars. I cashed it at the post office and managed to spend the best part of it stocking up on bare necessities to see me through the next couple of weeks.

Found this in today's paper:

Knife man blinds pensioner

A maniac wielding a knife who assaulted a pensioner on Saturday night is being hunted by police.

Reginald Finney, 71, who has been the victim of two previous muggings, was attacked outside Barclay's Bank, High Street, Whiteford, London E19.

A passing bus driver alerted the police and Mr Finney was taken to hospital with horrific injuries.

Police said that the knife-man attacked after watching Mr Finney withdraw money from the cash machine on Saturday night.

Search

The leather-jacketed attacker, believed to be in his mid-twenties with dark hair, was seen running in the direction of Grove Road shortly after the attack.

Police sealed off the area within twenty minutes of the call and officers have been carrying out door-to-door enquiries.

A spokesman said: 'This man is extremely dangerous. If anyone knows anything they should not hesitate to contact us. This is a very serious incident. There is no telling what this person might do next.'

They appear to have forgotten to mention that the knife, which is presently hidden in my wardrobe, belonged to Mr Finney.

Tuesday 30ᵗʰ January

Breakfast this morning was courtesy of Lena and consisted of a couple of slices of well-grilled, Swedish breast. I washed it down with a large vodka and orange. I offered Lena a sample of my cooking but she stared blankly at me with her remaining eye, not even daring to offer a thank-you when I later spooned a little into her open mouth. Ungrateful bitch! Although I guess it's a little difficult to talk when your tongue is stapled down. I couldn't be bothered putting her back up in the crucifixion position. It would be a waste of effort. She's not going anywhere now.

Wednesday 31ˢᵗ January

Went down the pub where I let Alison buy me lunch; pasty and chips.

Obviously in a mood to talk, Alison loitered around my table while I ate. This upset McCarthy - the old bloke that's owned the joint for the past twelve years - and he ordered Alison to collect in all the glasses and wipe down the tables. Not that I could give a shit, but the old faggot gets on my nerves.

Saturday 3ʳᵈ February

Pipes frozen again. I went next door to ask the old bat if I could fill my kettle. After ten minutes standing outside her door, in a vain attempt at convincing her that I wasn't one of the local yobs, my patience waned. I kicked the door in, grabbed her in a headlock and broke her neck. Having filled the kettle and after a brief nose around the old bat's apartment – finding a couple of hundred quid tucked in a coffee jar in her wardrobe – I pulled the door shut on her frail corpse.

Alison wants to see me tonight. I'll give it some thought!

Sunday 4ᵗʰ February

Gave Alison one last night.

I arrived at the pub ten minutes late looking slightly dishevelled and my shirt spotted with blood, though not mine, having had a bit of bother with a couple of would-be muggers from our estate shortly after leaving the apartment. Buying a drink from the spinster, I joined Alison in one of the booths and we spent the evening reminiscing over the couple of months we've been together. As the evening progressed and she became more and more intoxicated, Alison found it increasingly difficult to restrain her feelings. By the time we got back to her place, she was all over me. I'd barely helped her through the door of her bedsit before she stepped out of her shoes and was lifting the dress up over her head. Naturally, I wasn't going to turn down such an opportunity, and within seconds I stripped down to the polka dot boxer shorts that I was wearing beneath my jeans. She was like a dog on heat; she couldn't get enough!

Tuesday 6th February

No sign of Alison at work today. Returning to the flat, I found a message from her on the answer-phone. She wants me to call her. I'll give her a ring tomorrow.

Checking up on Lena, I found her on the floor curled up in a foetal position, her skin pale, a small trickle of blood running from her mouth. I kicked her in the stomach but there wasn't so much as a flinch. Her days are definitely numbered. I think I'll make tomorrow her last.

Wednesday 7th February

Alison is pregnant. Eight weeks to be precise. She obviously misinterpreted one night of sex as meaning something more. She couldn't wait for me to phone; she came over and delivered the news to my face first thing this morning. I didn't give her a chance to explain; I told her to get out of my sight and slammed the door in her face. An hour later, I was down the off-license taking a bottle of vodka. Unfortunately the proprietor gave chase when I walked out without paying. I had to go back to the store a few minutes later and remove a second bottle from the shelf after smashing the first one across the back of the man's head. I expect he'll recover. He wasn't bleeding too profusely when I left him. Unfortunately, I won't be able to use that off licence for the foreseeable future.

On my return, I went to the bathroom and retrieved the syringe and accompanying sachets. Five minutes later, having dragged Lena into the sitting room and administered a lethal cocktail of drugs, I poured myself a large drink, sat back in a chair and waited for the insane screaming to begin. I plan on spending the remainder of the day getting absolutely pissed out of my skull while watching Lena die a slow, excruciatingly painful death.

Thursday 8th February

Awakening with the effects of too much alcohol, I managed to tumble out of bed and reach the bathroom in time to stick my head down the porcelain bowl before throwing my guts up.

Having rinsed out my mouth I went into the sitting room, where I prodded my guest's head with my toe. Nothing. I knelt down beside her and checked for a pulse. Still nothing. There was no doubt about it: she was dead. I stood up, turned on the television and crossed the room to discover a message on the answer-phone from my brother Carl, wishing me a belated 'happy birthday'. Not bad – only about a month late, his excuse being that he was up to his neck with work and forgot all about it. I didn't bother to ring him back; there was little point, as we almost always end up arguing. I deleted the message and went back to bed. I'll sort Lena out later, it's not as if she's going anywhere.

Friday 9th February

With a gale blowing outside I didn't feel like going out, but I needed a new blade for my electric saw. It was therefore with some trepidation that I washed and dressed, then trudged the mile or so in the biting wind to the hardware store.

When I returned I found a note pushed beneath the door. It was from Alison. She wants to talk. She obviously can't take a hint. Well she can take a running jump!

Saturday 10th February

Sometime around eight last night I finally finished dissecting Lena's body and bagging the pieces I wanted, ready for the freezer. I buried the remains in the old refuse landfill site on the far bank of the canal. It's unlikely to be disturbed there. Cleaning up the blood and sinew in the bathroom where I had undertaken the task, I was feeling parched. After a quick shower I dressed and got to Bonaparte's for midnight. There, I soon caught sight of a couple of attractive women; one with dark hair, the other a peroxide blonde. Using the nearest telephone, I dialled the number for their table. Peroxide Blonde answered.

'Fancy giving us a blow job?' I asked.

'Fuck you, creep.'

I hung up before she could catch me with the receiver in my hand. Bitch. At closing time the pair left together and I was pleasantly surprised to discover that they were taking the same route home as me. Maintaining a safe distance behind the pair and keeping to the shadows, I followed for about half a mile before the older, black haired girl made her farewells, turned left and headed off in the direction of the tube station. I waited a few moments before continuing after Peroxide Blonde. My intention was to show her exactly what she was missing when she' rebuffed me earlier. Increasing my step to close the distance between us, I could feel the pressure of my erection straining against my trousers. I was about to reach out and grab her around the throat, to drag her into the narrow alley that leads to the estate, when someone called out behind us. My quarry stopped in her tracks. I barely prevented myself from colliding with her. Glancing around to see who it was that had interfered with my plans, I saw Peroxide Blonde's companion running towards us. Quickly, I sank back into the shadows and began walking from the scene, any plans that I might have had for the night, forgotten. As I moved away, I heard the dark haired girl mention something about forgetting her keys ... Of all the luck!

This evening I spent sat in front of the television, only stepping out around ten-thirty for a burger from the take-away van parked down the road. I wish I hadn't bothered; it was still raw in the middle and tasted like shit.

Wednesday 14th February
Valentine's Day

Felt like crap the past couple of days, confined to bed with stomach cramps and nausea. It doesn't take a doctor to realise that I'm suffering from a dose of food poisoning. When I get my hands on that son of a bitch who owns the burger van, he will have a hell of a lot of explaining to do. Bastard!
    Received a card in the post. The writing could only belong to one person I know: Alison. The inscription was short and to the point: 'Love you always'. I tore the card up and threw it in the bin. I don't have the patience for emotional, pregnant sluts at the moment.

7.30 pm Just eaten a couple of slices of toast. The first thing I've had in four days.

Friday 16th February

Torched the burger van. The place was a pigsty. Unwashed utensils lay on the hot plate; the bin was full to overflowing; remnants of food had been trodden into the greasy, rotting floor where they had fallen; and cockroaches scurried uninhibited across the work surfaces. It was unbelievable. Fortunately for the fat bastard himself, he was not there, else I might have found great enjoyment in ramming a petrol soaked newspaper up his ass and igniting it.

Saturday 17th February

Went to the barbers for a trim. Quite a pleasant experience for a change. Instead of the Greek owner rubbing his crotch against my elbow whenever the opportunity arose, there was some new girl who was totally oblivious to the fact that she was grinding her luscious ripe breasts into my face. I couldn't think of anything better than kissing and sucking those beautiful examples of womanhood. I left, leaving her a tip and my number; you never know, she may call!

When I returned to the flat, I noticed the door to the old bat's place adjacent to mine was slightly ajar. Intrigued, I pushed it open a little further and was surprised to see one of the local yobs from the estate - he couldn't have been older than fifteen – going through the old bat's belongings. Obviously her decaying corpse had not deterred him. He was too engrossed in rifling through her property to notice me, so I pulled the door quietly to and went back downstairs to a nearby phone box and called the police anonymously. The plan worked. Fifteen minutes later the police were leading the youth away in handcuffs, while a medic examined the corpse. It wouldn't take much for them to realize that she had been dead for a couple of weeks, but the youth would be in for a hard time explaining his presence in the flat in the first place, let alone convincing the authorities that he wasn't responsible for the woman's death on an earlier occasion. I was asked a few routine questions, but that was all they were – routine – and I wasn't too concerned.

Monday 19th February

Alison pushed me one step too far this evening.

I was having a quiet drink in the Dog and Duck when Andrew arrived. Getting himself a pint and a refill for me, he asked if I fancied going to Bonaparte's: 'They're holding a stag party this evening,' he said. Bonaparte's stag nights are legendary, for all the wrong reasons, and I certainly wasn't going to say no to such an opportunity. The action started about an hour later when the four ripe, scantily clad and very attractive young women got onto the dance floor. The entire room was awestricken as they performed lurid, sexually suggestive acts on themselves and a few fortunate customers. These events rarely go without hitch, particularly at Bonaparte's. With well over three hundred hot blooded males packed in a confined space and all drooling over the same four women, the problems were obvious. Before long a brawl started, and the baseball bats were wielded as the bouncers stormed in to defuse the situation. Losing Andrew in the madness that followed, as fights broke out around the room I joined in with the fun, kneeing one bloke in the groin before slamming his nose back up into his skull. When the sound of the sirens announced the premature arrival of the police, I dragged a burly biker from Andrew's instantly recognisable form and slammed his head into the bar counter to save Andrew from receiving another pounding from his assailant's fist. Outside, Andrew, sporting a bloody nose, was more concerned about losing his mobile phone in the commotion than anything else. I helped him into a passing taxi and sent him on his way. He offered me a lift, but I declined. Still fuelled by the adrenalin flowing through my system, I was hoping to find some action on the way home. Little did I know at that point that Alison would be on the receiving end!

I was walking back to my apartment, coming up the road that leads to the Dog and Duck, when just ahead of me I caught sight of two figures, apparently arguing, outside the travel agent's. As I drew closer, a car drove past and sounded its horn. Both the figures looked around and one of them waved. It was Alison. She had obviously finished work. I could vaguely make out that the person with her was also a woman, although I didn't recognize her. If there was one person I didn't want to see tonight it was Alison, especially the mood I was in. Unfortunately, Alison spotted me. Her head nodded towards me, and her companion glanced over in my direction. I turned back the way I'd come and quickly headed across the park, taking the gravel path that runs in the direction of the lake. It wasn't long before I heard the sound of Alison's shoes on the loose stones as she came after me.

'Saul,' she called out from behind me, her voice breaking the night silence.

I continued walking. I didn't want to know.

'Don't you fucking walk away from me,' she continued, grabbing me by the arm and preventing me from going on. 'I want to talk to you.'

'Piss off and leave me alone.'

She wouldn't leave it alone. 'I will not. What is it with you these days?'

'What is it with me? How dare you. You stupid, stupid bitch … look at you. You spend a week with your ex on some lame excuse and then come back home and announce that you're pregnant. Something that I wouldn't be particularly happy to hear at the best of times. But do you seriously expect me to believe that it's mine? You can go back to him. He's welcome to you for all I care. I'm sure the three of you will be very happy together. A nice little family.'

Alison was near to tears. 'Saul, you don't understand. It wasn't like that. The baby's yours. I swear on my life.'

'That's fortunate for you. Let's see if it does you any good!'

A soft gasp of air passed Alison's lips. A shocked expression crossed her face. She looked down at my hand as I withdrew the blade of the flick-knife from her stomach. Before she could say anything, I plunged the knife into her a second time and a then a third, twisting the blade each time and forcing it in further to ensure that it hit home. A scream began to surface from the depths of her soul, but as I sliced her throat open it was replaced by a gurgling sound.

Alison collapsed at my feet.

I knelt down beside her and made certain she was dead before wiping the knife on her sleeve and folding it back into the handle, careful not to cut myself on the over-sharpened blade. I then returned the weapon to my jacket pocket, where it has a permanent home; ready at a moment's notice for incidents such as this.

Tuesday 20ᵗʰ February

Alison's body was found at five-thirty this morning. Police believe that she was attacked not long after leaving the pub. At the moment they have no idea of a motive. With a bit of luck it will remain that way.

Wednesday 21ˢᵗ February

Found Andrew in the pub this afternoon, having a late lunch. He's heard about Alison, which is hardly surprising under the circumstances. She's managed to make the news morning, noon and night since her body was found early yesterday.

'I can't understand how you can remain so calm about the death of your girlfriend,' Andrew said, while McCarthy glared at me from behind the two feet of mahogany as he poured me a pint.

'Ex!' I answered him, taking the pint from McCarthy and handing over the correct change. 'We'd split up.' I took a sip of my beer. 'As it happens, I would prefer not to discuss the matter.' That was the end of the subject as far as Andrew was concerned, but I could sense McCarthy maintaining a suspicious eye on me from his vantage point behind the bar. Not something he wants to continue with if he plans to reach retirement age intact.

Thursday 22ⁿᵈ February

More news on Alison:

HUNT FOR BARMAID'S KILLER CONTINUES …

Detectives hunting the killer of barmaid Alison Lewis last night appealed for a woman seen talking to her outside the Amigar Travel Agency in Shipton Road, during the early hours of Monday morning.

They want the woman, dressed in jeans and pale blouse and with reddish hair, to come forward to help with their enquiries.

Alison, 23, was brutally murdered after leaving the Dog & Duck pub in Chapel Street, where she worked. The murder weapon has yet to be retrieved.

I'm intrigued to know who the woman was.

Friday 23ʳᵈ February

Had a courteous visit from the local constabulary. They have finally linked me to Alison; probably after a phone call or two from McCarthy, I wouldn't be surprised. I think a word in his ear is definitely in order. I can't have people spreading idle gossip about me, can I!

After a brief, but thorough, line of questioning I was more than confident that I had convinced the over zealous Sergeant that I didn't really know Alison and, although I'd been out with her once or twice, it hadn't worked out.

Weathermen have warned that there is an exceptionally cold spell moving in over the next couple of days. Joy of joys. I will look forward to that. Not!

Saturday 24th February

A storm is raging overhead. Rain is falling in torrents, beating against the windows. The lightening flashes and claps of thunder are mere seconds apart. From the window I can see the afternoon shoppers scurrying like ants for cover.

I received my giro in the post, but decided against going out to cash it because of the weather. On the lunchtime news the reporter said that a woman had been taken in for questioning late last night over Alison's murder. A case of being in the right place at the wrong time, I'd say!

Sunday 25th February

Went down the video shop last night and took out a couple of the *Nightmare on Elm Street* films. It's been a long time since I first saw them and they're still great fun.

The weather was still bad, and by the time I returned home it had started to snow, although not heavily.

I went down the pub at lunchtime for a couple of pints, and the spinster informed me that Alison's funeral is on Tuesday. To be honest I hadn't even given it a thought, but then I suppose everyone is entitled to a funeral of some form or another. I guess I should make an appearance or some may consider it a little suspicious.

Monday 26th February

In the paper there was a small article about Alison. The woman helping police with their enquiries has now been released without charge. Who she is and what she was doing in the area I have not the faintest idea. I assume this was the same woman I saw talking to Alison before she followed me to the park. If so, it begs the question why I haven't heard more than I have from the police. Evidently they are no nearer to solving Alison's murder.

Tuesday 27th February
Shrove Tuesday

Alison was buried today. It's a week since I sliced her up, and the police are still running around like headless chickens. I decided to put in an appearance at the funeral. I couldn't be bothered with the buses and, although it's not insured, decided to take the Prelude out. As it happens, there were very few people there, and thankfully the service was short and to the point. At the front were an elderly couple, dressed in traditional funeral black. I vaguely remember seeing a photo of them in Alison's bedsit, and can only assume them to be her parents. Next to them stood a woman who must have been another relative; perhaps her sister, though I didn't get a good look at her as her face was obscured by the veil she wore over her hat. McCarthy had given himself time off from the pub to make his presence known. Surprisingly enough he had given the spinster the session off as well, although I expect he's probably docked her pay for the privilege. Last but not least, there were two representatives of the police force keeping a watchful eye over the proceedings, making a mental note of those who had attended and just as likely those who hadn't.

As I was leaving, I collided with the veiled woman; intentionally on her part, I think. She glared at me through her veil until I stepped around her, but even as I started the car I could see her reflection in the wing mirror while she stood in the middle of the cemetery car park. She was still staring after me as I drove away. Weird!

Wednesday 28th February

Got up early and went for a walk in the park. It was cold, but I needed to get some fresh air into my lungs. For some reason I couldn't sleep much last night, and by this morning the dreariness of my apartment was getting to me.

Taking the path around the lake, I was a little surprised to see a pair of uniformed figures walking in my direction. It's been nine days now since Alison crossed me, and during that time the police have been unable to come up with anything. Consequently, seeing two constables - one of them female - making their way towards me along the same route I took on that fateful night caught me momentarily off guard. I needn't have worried though; they were on nothing more than a routine patrol and didn't give me a second glance. The WPC was a right stunner. I could have given her one there and then if she had been on her own. Come to think of it, I've always wanted a girl in uniform; could be a bit of a turn on, and I could certainly make use of the handcuffs. I'll keep an eye out for her in the future.

Thursday 1st March

I've lost my wallet. I can't find it anywhere. Usually I leave it with my keys on the shelf in the hall, but it's not there. Thinking about it now, I haven't seen it for a day or two. I know I had it when I went to Alison's funeral, because I had to stop at the garage on the way there to fill up with petrol. I can't remember if I had it after that though. I've checked the jacket I was wearing on Tuesday, but with no joy. It's not just the money I'm annoyed about - there was probably thirty quid in there, I think - but it's got my driving licence and bank and membership cards. It means I will have to go through the hassle of cancelling the lot.

Friday 2nd March

Cancelled my cards and ordered replacements. I'll have a chat with the receptionist at Bonaparte's next time I go there to get a replacement membership card. I've also had to send off for a duplicate driving license. Knowing my luck, the wallet will turn up tomorrow.

Saturday 3rd March

No wallet; it was a slim hope anyway. However, I received a very unusual note in the post today:

saul roberts

have no doubt that i know who you are and where you live and that i am coming for you if the authorities don't catch up with you then i guarantee that i will spare you not the pain and suffering you have already inflicted upon me. watching you always

It was unsigned. Attached was a small cutting from the local paper. As it happens, it was one I must have missed:

Killer still at large …

The killer of pregnant barmaid Alison Lewis is still at large. A police spokesman stated: 'Due to the viciousness of this attack, it is imperative that we apprehend the culprit as quickly as possible. If there is anyone that has any information regarding this crime, they should contact us immediately.'

I didn't like the way that the last sentence had been heavily underlined.

Tuesday 6th March

I've got a new girlfriend!

The Dog and Duck was pretty much empty when I arrived, so it didn't take me long to notice that the woman sat at the bar was on her own. In her early twenties, she was dressed in blue Levi's that clung tightly to her long, slender legs and a silk blouse that, hanging off the shoulder with the first three buttons undone, stirred the imagination appreciably. As she flicked her long dark hair from her face, I caught sight of her sparkling blue eyes and foolishly realised that she had been making her own appraisals. After a brief introduction, I discovered that her name was Laura. We talked for a while and she revealed that she was a model, mainly doing catalogue work. She is due to fly abroad for a calendar shoot at the end of the month.

'What brings you to a place like this on a Tuesday afternoon?' I asked. 'It's off the beaten track a bit; for a jet-setting model, that is!'

'We've all got to start somewhere,' she answered. 'As it happens, my parents don't live too far from here. I've been staying with them for a while. I needed to get out of the house, and I guess I just landed up here.'

'I know the feeling, though usually I find that it's after I've had a few drinks that I'm not quire sure how I got someplace, not on my way to the pub.'

Laura smiled. 'We have a comedian in our midst, I see!'

And so the conversation continued until Laura received a call on her mobile phone. After she had knocked back her drink, we made our farewells; although not before arranging to see each other again on Thursday.

Thursday 8ᵗʰ March

Met Laura at Leicester Square. After a couple of drinks in one of the locals, we wandered up Charing Cross Road to catch the afternoon performance of some new musical that's recently opened. Laura's treat. Though the music and costumes were good, it wasn't my cup of tea. In fact, an apt description would be three hours of bum-numbing boredom; but then, that's my opinion. Laura, on the other hand, thought it was great; the best show she'd seen in months. I hope she doesn't take it upon herself to buy tickets for anything else, because she's only going to be upset when I tell her where to stick them!

Friday 9ᵗʰ March

Laura's out on some promotional work in the city with her friend Melanie, but she promised to call as soon as they've both finished.

Saturday 10ᵗʰ March

Last night Laura slept over; she had the bed and I suffered the indignity of the floor; the sofa is far too uncomfortable. I thought everything was going smoothly. One moment she was all kisses and cuddles, the next she was distant and cold and wouldn't let me touch her. I felt that I was under scrutiny. Needless to say I considered the options. But I decided against making any rash decisions until I've been able to determine which way the land lies.

I picked her up at seven from her parents' house, a four bedroom Victorian detached with views of the golf course, where I was introduced to her father, the Reverend Richardson. His profession took me totally by surprise. Men of the cloth always seem to set my hair up on end, and they are not my favourite group of people. Her mother is still working; she's a volunteer for the Samaritans. I've probably spoken to her in the past. Taking the tube into the city, we went to a cosy little restaurant in Chinatown. Later, we moved on to the Hippodrome, where Laura danced the night away while I propped up one of the bars, making sure that no-one tried to intrude on my territory. There was some charity event going on, and the television cameras were waiting in abundance to catch the guest celebrities as they arrived with their entourages. Unfortunately the cameras were turned in the opposite direction when we walked in. It would have been fun to see ourselves on television. Not unsurprisingly, I was stopped at the door, but Laura flashed her VIP card and the doormen grudgingly let me pass.

I'm seeing Laura again on Monday.

Monday 12ᵗʰ March

After a cold shower, the ancient immersion heater having given up its struggle with a loud explosion a few days ago, I hurried to meet Laura at the Dog and Duck. She wasn't there when I arrived, so I got the round in – a pint of lager for me and an orange juice for her – and set the glasses down on the table nearest the door. She arrived a moment later, gasping for breath.

Her bedraggled appearance startled me, but she explained that she had been ready to leave the house when the phone rang. It was the modelling agency. They've got both Melanie and her an extra shoot in New York, but they've got to fly out at the end of the week. Their flight will be confirmed on Friday.

Laura had driven to the pub as fast as she could to tell me her news, but the traffic had been slow. After she had eventually found herself a parking space further up the road, it had begun to rain, and she had got soaked.

I listened to all of this in a daze. It leaves us with not much time together, and I still haven't shagged her. Later on, after a bite to eat and a bottle of champagne to celebrate her good fortune, Laura took the bus back to her parents' house. I promised to return her car, a BMW convertible, when I'd sobered up.

27

Wednesday 14ᵗʰ March

Sabrina, Laura's sister, has told her about a new nightclub opening in the city next week. Laura suggested I apply for a job. My immediate response was unfavourable to say the least. It's been a couple of years since I last served behind a bar; and, after the fire that resulted in the deaths of the landlord and his family, I swore I'd never do it again. Now, with further thought, it doesn't seem such a bad idea. After all, if that landlord hadn't taken it upon himself to dismiss me for pounding a customer (his brother), I wouldn't have dropped the match on his petrol-soaked bed while he slept.

4.30 pm Phoned the club and arranged an interview for tomorrow at midday.

Thursday 15ᵗʰ March

Arrived for the interview with twenty minutes to spare. The club is called the Ritzavoy and is situated around the corner from Stringfellow's, in Long Acre.

There were three others awaiting an interview so I had time to take in the glitzy decor around me. It follows the basic discotheque design: a central dance floor; a main bar situated close to the reception and cloakroom; a smaller cocktail bar at the other end of the club; and, through an archway, the restaurant. To be honest, it is quite impressive, and obviously a large sum of money has been invested in the place.

Once I'd completed my application form, the interview lasted for fifteen to twenty minutes. Simon Lloyd, the manager, said that they were looking for bar staff with character rather than experience. I don't know how he rated me, but he said he would give me a call tomorrow and let me know.

I phoned Laura immediately and, after a couple of drinks at the pub, we picked up a pizza from the take-away and came back home. Later, as I was savouring the taste of my last mouthful of cheese and pepperoni, she took me unawares when she calmly looked up from her cross-legged position on the floor and asked if I wanted to make love to her. Such was my surprise that my mouth dropped open. I must have mumbled some form of reply, for she rose to her feet and crossed the room to the bed. Not wanting to miss out on the opportunity, I quickly stripped off and joined her.

Result!

Friday 16ᵗʰ March

Laura arrived at lunchtime, with Melanie in tow.

The pair together are ultimate stunners and could easily be mistaken for sisters. I would have no hesitation in giving Melanie one any day. She is one of the most flirtatious people I have ever met, and that's saying something.

28

According to Laura, Melanie will get so wrapped up with a bloke that he won't know what hit him until it's too late. Laura told me that their flight has been confirmed. They are due to depart from Heathrow at seven-thirty on Sunday morning. Which doesn't leave me that much time with Laura. No news about the job.

Saturday 17th March

Popped into town to stock up on a few provisions. On returning, I had the oddest sensation that someone had been in the apartment while I was out. I had a look about the place and although everything appears to be in order I can't get it out of my head that someone has been nosing around. If I discover who it was they will live to regret it!

I've got it; the job at the Ritzavoy. Lloyd's secretary phoned at ten-thirty and said that I start this Thursday. I'm to wear black trousers and shoes and they'll sort me out with a shirt when I arrive.

Sunday 18th March

Got Laura to the airport just in time. Melanie was waiting at the boarding gate, glancing anxiously at the clock as we ran up to meet her. As Laura kissed me goodbye I felt uncomfortable and realised that I was going to miss her. The postcards and letters that she promised to write will be little consolation so early in our relationship, but there's nothing I can do about it.

Wednesday 21st March

It pissed down last night, but although it sleeted for a while, there was no snow.

Found Andrew in the pub at lunchtime, apparently mourning the death of one of his regular punters. The stupid fool blew the back of his head off using a shotgun – an accident apparently, although what state of mind he was in at the time is anyone's guess. I've heard rumours that there's some bad gear on the market at the moment. It wouldn't surprise me if Andrew has picked some up on the cheap and is selling it on to make an extra-quick buck.

While I was with Andrew I noticed a man stood beside the bar. He had been in conversation with the spinster when I first walked in but, after I joined Andrew, his attention switched to me. He goes by the name of Laws; Inspector Laws. He's with the local CID, and I've had more than my share of run-ins with him in the past. He is not one to take lightly.

Thursday 22nd March

I start the new job tonight. I've got to be at the club by seven for an induction session. The doors open at nine for the VIP's with their free bar and then at ten for the regular nightclub clientele. I suppose that gives me a couple of hours to learn the prices.

Friday 23rd March

Started at the Ritzavoy last night. What a night for a club to open!. There was torrential rain most of the evening, although it didn't prevent the prospective customers from finding their way in. The queue was backed up to the Covent Garden underground by ten o'clock; by eleven, they'd closed the doors, only admitting people on the basis of one out, one in.

For the first night of working behind a new bar I did pretty well, even if I do say so myself. I made nearly twenty quid in tips and managed to pocket another fifty. I probably could have made a lot more if I'd thought about it, but the hours flew by. Admittedly, by the time the taxis arrived at three-thirty to take the staff home, I was falling asleep on my feet. I think the hours are going to take a little getting used to.

Saturday 24th March

Fucked myself up good and proper!

I was speaking to Alex last night. He is one of the club's two disc jockeys. 'A hundred and sixty-five sit-ups!' he said after I mentioned how many I'd done that morning. 'That's pathetic. I'm on two hundred at least, and a hundred plus press-ups!'

By the look of him, I doubt if he can manage fifty sit-ups let alone two hundred. The only exercise he gets is the verbal babble that he spouts; unfortunately he is also the one with the microphone and a seven-hundred-strong captive audience. Throughout the evening he was unrelenting with his barrage of wisecracks about my stamina. When I got home this morning I had reached the end of my tether. I sat on the floor and began the sit-ups; two hundred later, I fell back on the floor in agony. I must have strained a dozen or so muscles. I can barely stand upright. It would have been a damn sight easier to have slit the moron's fucking throat!

Sunday 25th March
Mothering Sunday.

May the bitch rest in peace! I would have sent her a card, if only to remind her that I existed, but having not seen her since she walked out on Carl and me when we were still infants, I have no idea where she is today. She could very well be dead for all I know. I still remember the look on our father's face when he came in from work one evening and read the note she had left him. From that moment on he was on a downward spiral; going from one relationship to another. Woman after woman took advantage of him, frittering away what little savings he had. The end, when it came, was hardly a surprise. He died a broken man, taking his own life a week after being diagnosed with syphilis; a pretty mild complaint these days, when you consider the alternatives. From that day on, I vowed that the same was never going to happen to me. No way was I going to let prick-teasing bitches take advantage of me!

I wonder how Laura is getting on. She should be sunning it up on a beach someplace by now. Wish I was with her; I hate this cold weather.

Given up on the exercise at the moment – I'm still in too much pain from overdoing the sit-ups the other night.

Tuesday 27th March

Andrew held a party last night. Sarah was there, and a number of others that I recognised both from the past and as acquaintances of Andrew. At one point there were about forty people packed in the front two rooms of his house. All of them were engaged in savouring various illicit substances that had been kindly provided by the host. I stayed on the beer. Around midnight I found Sarah spaced out on the bathroom floor. With Andrew out of the way, making sure his guests were well satisfied, I satisfied myself; removing my cock and lifting up Sarah's dress, I tore off her knickers and entered her. The state she was in, I might as well not have bothered. She didn't stir throughout; I've had more pleasure fucking a corpse.

The party continued on into the early hours of the morning, but a little after one I made my excuses and left.

Wednesday 28th March

Received a postcard from Laura:

March 23rd

Saul,

Having a great time so far. New York is just like you see it on television. The shoot was tiring but good fun; the money wasn't bad either. Barbados is wonderful. Two weeks here and then we fly to Crete. I'm off to the beach now, for another photo session, so I'll say goodbye.

Don't work too hard.

All my love,

Laura XXX

Glad to see she's enjoying herself.

Thursday 29th March

A new girl started in the cloakroom at the club last night. Her name is Sasha. Her blonde hair, almost down to her waist, and slender figure will put her at the top of my list any day; second only to Portia de Rossi who plays that ice-cool lawyer Nell in *Ally McBeal*. If Laura were at home in London I probably wouldn't bother with her - actually that's a complete lie, I wouldn't give a shit whether Laura was around or not!

Saturday 31st March

Joined some of the staff from the club for an after-work drink at Moody Blues: one of a number of illegal shenanigan-drinking establishments that occupy the London suburbs.

Tried to start up a conversation with Sasha but she was having none of it and even turned her back on me when I offered her a drink. Bitch! She may have started at the club a couple of days after the rest of us, but that's not the right attitude to have.

'When I'm interested I will let you know,' she said, slapping my hand away. 'In the meantime, I don't think my boyfriend would appreciate me sleeping around.'

I tried to convince her that she was wrong, but she wasn't interested.

With the sun beginning to invade the night sky and me having drunk half a bottle of an unknown brand of vodka, my head felt as if it was on a skydive to hell, closely followed by the contents of my stomach. I'm pretty sure that working at the club is going to be a lot of fun.

Tuesday 3rd April

Had a run-in with my old friend from the CID this morning!

Returning from a short trip down to the shops to pick up a few needed provisions, I noticed a figure that I recognized. He was in conversation with a woman outside the entrance to the flats. As I approached, the woman backed away and Inspector Laws held open the door into the foyer.

'Good morning, Mr Roberts,' he said, following me into the building. 'It's been quite a while since we last spoke, so I thought I'd come and see how you are doing.'

'Is this an official visit, or can I tell you to go screw yourself?' I pressed the button for the lift and waited.

'I don't think that would be wise, do you?' He glanced around, his nostrils flaring at the stench of urine that is forever present and that I barely notice these days. 'It was an unfortunate incident with that young lady from the pub, wasn't it? What was her name? Alison, wasn't it? Was she any good in bed?' He paused while he removed a notebook from his pocket and glanced quickly through its pages. 'Of course, you wouldn't have any idea, would you, because you didn't really know her. Shame. Someone did, and they evidently knew her well enough to get her in the family way, if you know what I mean.'

I glanced up at the lights above the elevator doors. The lift was at the fifth floor. Though slow, it was at least working.

'I thought perhaps that as you are quite a frequent visitor to the Dog and Duck, you might have seen her with someone or heard something on the grapevine that you would be willing to share with me.'

'You wish.'

Laws smiled: 'It was worth a try. You never know when someone from the past might prove to do you a good turn later down the road.'

The doors to the elevator opened. I stepped inside and pressed the button for the tenth floor. Laws didn't follow, but reached out at the last minute to prevent the door closing.

'Funny business that, with this old thing, last October.' His fingers tapped the side of the open door.

'In what way?'

'Well … don't you think it odd that the engineers couldn't find anything wrong with either of the lifts and yet that young man still fell to his death?'

'Not my problem, is it?' I answered. I knew the full details of incident to which he was referring, but wasn't planning on sharing them any time soon. 'They're working at the moment, which is all I'm concerned with.'

'Hmmm, I guess you're right! Mind you, the coroner reckons he must have fallen a hundred and twenty feet, give or take. That would have put him on the tenth floor, where you live.' His eyes fixed on mine. ' If I were you, I wouldn't go leaning on those doors … It's better to be safe than sorry.'

'Thanks for the advice.'

'No problem.'

Laws removed his hand and the doors began to close, leaving me to ascend on my own with my thoughts. It's unlikely that this morning's visit will be the last I see of Inspector Laws.

Friday 6th April

Another card from Laura:

> *April 2nd*
>
> *Saul,*
>
> *Just a quickie to tell you about Melanie; she's only gone and got herself engaged to some American yachtie-type! Ring and all. I haven't met him yet, but I will give you the full juicy details when I have.*
>
> *Love*
>
> *Laura XXXX*

I've decided that now's the time to move. I should have enough money to put down for a deposit on a decent flat in a more salubrious area of town. With a bit of luck, it might act as a suitable temptation for Laura to move in with me on her return.

Sunday 8th April

Laura phoned. Reverse charge from Crete. She's got some front!
   Apparently Melanie had a big bust up with her fiancée after she discovered him in bed with his current wife. She has locked herself in her room and hasn't been out for days. 'The agency are fuming,' Laura said. I probed her for the dates of her return, but she didn't know. She thought it could be as long as a month; the agency are continually finding them additional bookings all the time and the work is flowing in. As far as Laura is aware, both she and Mel will remain in Crete, with the exception of a couple of days at the beginning of next week when they're due to be in Rhodes. What a life she leads!

Monday 9th April

Bought the local papers in an attempt to find better accommodation. Came up with one possibility and made an appointment to view it at 2 pm.

3.30 pm In my entire life I have never come across accommodation any worse than my current abode. Until this afternoon, that is! The small dingy room I visited was better suited to the rats and beetles that scurried across the floor when I shoved the door open. The naked floorboards were rotten and the alcove that pretended to be a kitchen was strewn with ancient litter. The single bulb, hanging from naked cables, provided barely enough light, leaving the majority of the cracked, plastered walls in shadow. If that wasn't bad enough, the landlord suggested that the rent would be almost twice what I'm paying for this place. To cap it all, he wanted two months' payment up front. By the time he told me this I was unable to restrain myself any longer, and rolled up in a fit of laughter.

The thought of leaving the arrogant git lying sprawled on the floor, his skull crushed by a blow to the back of his head with the frying pan left by a previous occupant, was not far from my mind. Reluctantly, I denied myself the pleasure and told him where he could stick his rent, before walking out and leaving him to it.

Tuesday 10th April

Phoned up a number of property agents. They're sending me a list of one-bedroom flats that are currently available. Should have more luck than with the papers.

Wednesday 11th April

Received the details of a prospective flat through the post. I've arranged to view it tomorrow.

Thursday 12th April

Saw the flat this morning. It's just what I'm looking for. A ground floor flat, one bedroom with en suite bathroom, large lounge with patio doors that open out onto the rear garden, and a separate kitchen. The furniture, although well used, is clean and comfortable. It's in a much better area than I currently live. Best of all, it's not much more than what I'm already paying.

I told the agent that I needed a couple of days to think about it, but my mind is already made up.

Saturday 14th April

Lloyd almost caught me giving out free drinks to a couple of women I was chatting to this evening. Fortunately Lisa rang a round into the till a moment after he stepped behind the bar and he couldn't prove anything.

Monday 16th April
Bank Holiday Monday.

Spent the entire day giving the car a good strip down, wash and polish. It's now nine-thirty and I've finished. I've had the Prelude for nearly five years and, although there's over a hundred and sixty thousand on the clock, it still drives like a dream. Unfortunately, my recent lack of finances has meant it has been off the road more often than on. However, I intend on changing that. All I need do now is sort out the tax etc, so that I will be legal and above-board.

Tuesday 17th April

Poured with rain all day.

Phoned the property agent and told him that I've decided to take the flat. After the call, I wrote out a cheque to cover the deposit and first month's rent and put it in the post to him. I can pick the keys up from the office next week, once the cheque has cleared.

Went with Andrew for a drink down the Dog and Duck. He had a meeting with a new supplier. It was lucky for him that I'd agreed to go along. I recognised his supposed supplier immediately. It was none other than an associate of my old friend Inspector Laws. Much to his disappointment, he and his three undercover colleagues left the pub empty handed.

Wednesday 18th April

The gall of some people! There I was waiting for the tube at Bank when a woman, probably in her mid-thirties, rattling a tin in front of my face and demanding change, interrupted my thoughts. She barely realised that she'd caught my attention when I angrily told her where to go. She rattled the tin a moment longer, then went on her way; only to be replaced seconds later by a young girl tugging at my sleeve, repeating her mother's plea. It was then that the train pulled into the station. Not even the driver would have noticed if I'd shoved the youngster off the platform and into the vehicle's path. And I would have done it, had her mother not grabbed her by the arm and dragged her off, leaving an assault of verbal abuse in her wake, which gave an indication of her displeasure.

The language people use in front of their kids these days!

Thursday 19th April

About to leave the building this morning, I caught the postman and was pleasantly surprised when he handed me an airmail envelope, though it was postmarked in England. I tore it open and found two pages of thin blue paper written in Laura's neat hand.

18th April

Crete.

Saul,

It's all your fault – I've just banged myself twice, hard – once on my knee and once on my elbow – rushing about the apartment so that I've got time to write to you.

Melanie is out by the pool for a photo session at the moment. I don't have to be there for another forty minutes, so I thought I'd let you know what's been going on since I spoke to you last week.

The weather here is milder than in Barbados; still plenty of sun but not as hot. It's hard to believe that it's only April. You'd love it here.

We returned from Rhodes late last night - on our own private yacht. (There was Melanie, me, Carol and Janet – who is flying home this afternoon and has promised to post this letter.) We had a great time; spent only three hours in front of the camera during the three days we were there. The rest of the time we used for sightseeing. Since we first arrived in Crete, Melanie has been pining for her yachtie bloke – even phoned him a couple of times. At one stage we all thought she had forgiven him and was about to pack up her modelling and fly back to Barbados to see him, wife and all. Luckily, the night before she was due to fly back, she met a bronzed hunk of a Greek who took her fancy immediately. His friend wasn't bad either - only joking. By the end of the night she had forgotten all about her ex-fiancée. Instead she's meeting the hunk after her shoot this afternoon.

I'm going to have to go now. Janet has just popped her head around the door and said that she'll be leaving in a couple of minutes.

Catch you soon.

Miss you lots.

Love,

Laura

I hope she is only joking about the bronzed Greeks. If I ever hear that she's been cheating on me she'll regret it for the remainder of what will surely be a very short life.

Friday 20th April

Enigma Electric Tour. Four beautiful young blondes dancing to the sounds of yesteryear with a dazzling laser show going on around them. The highlight of the evening was the brunette – a twenty year old art student by the name of Debbie – who had been coming on to me most of the evening to score herself some free drinks.

After work, I met the brunette outside the club and we caught a taxi back here. While she was in the bathroom I slipped a copy of *The Exorcist* into the video and sat down with a bottle of beer. When she came into the lounge she looked a little disappointed at seeing the television on, but it wasn't long before she was kneeling between my legs, her head bobbing up and down in my lap as I relaxed to watch the film. Later, after the film had finished, I went for a piss while she got into bed. Shortly after, the screaming began!

38

Saturday 21st April

The bed linen is beyond redemption. The brunette wouldn't stop bleeding. I spent the entire morning cleaning up after her. Around eight this morning, having wrapped the corpse in the stained sheets, I managed to drag the body down to the car, unobserved, and drove out to the old tip, only to change my mind rather hastily when I found forty or so cars and the start of a crowd beginning to mill about. Of all the days to choose; there was a car boot sale close to the spot I've been using. The possibility of being seen was too great. Instead I drove out of town to a small grouping of trees next to the motorway junction and an old drainage service outlet that I've used in the past. The surrounding land is waterlogged and the outlet itself is in two feet of water; enough of a deterrent to deter the odd passer-by from taking an interest!

Monday 23rd April

Went to pick up the keys to the flat and was annoyed to be fobbed off with a lame excuse from the agent to the effect that someone had misplaced the paperwork and that until it is found I am unable to move in. In other words, they've had a better offer on the place. I left with the agent promising to call me as soon as the problem has been resolved. He better had!

Met Sasha for a drink up the West End. She and her boyfriend are not getting on at the moment, so I took advantage of the situation. Unfortunately she wasn't in much of a mood for company. In the end I made an excuse and left her to it.

Tuesday 24th April

Nothing much going on. Still annoyed that I can't move in to the new place, so I spent the day indoors compiling a list of a few of my pet hates:

- Kids
- Pregnant women – they produce kids
- Liars
- Street beggars and their children
- The cold weather
- Bills – usually because they want my money
- Lateness
- Obnoxious disc jockeys such as Alex
- Property agents who don't deliver

The property agents could well move to the top of my list if they don't come up with the keys.

Wednesday 25th April

Had an evening off last night, and having already given some thought to my pet hates, I came up with a list of my favourite things, although I'm sure I've missed a few:

- A good shag at least four times a day
- Details of a good juicy disaster
- Cherry pie and custard – haven't had that for a while!
- The Simpsons
- Budweiser – substitutes okay
- Grilled heart with a pleasant red wine
- Intestines – well boiled
- Money and plenty of it
- Cemeteries
- Sunnier climates
- A good Chinese takeaway
- Blondes

Wouldn't life be bliss if I found myself a blonde nymphomaniac with plenty of cash in the bank, who enjoyed a Chinese and had no objection to making love in a cemetery. In the meantime I'll stick with Laura; as long as she comes back, that is!

Thursday 26th April

Didn't awake until nearly midday. When I did eventually rise from my bed I was glad to find, besides the bills, another card from Laura:

April 21st

Saul,

Hope you are coping without me!
The weather has changed for the worse since Wednesday. It's now pouring with rain and there's the threat of a storm. Reminds me of England. Don't ask me what the picture on the front is, I haven't a clue. We've got a few days off next weekend. Some of the girls are

*planning on going home. I thought about it and can't
wait to see you again, but I expect I'll stay here and do
some sightseeing. Anyway, time to go.*

Thinking of you always.

Lots of Love,

Laura XXXXX

I turned the card over and looked at the photograph on the front. I could see what she meant. The photograph of a stone statue with a small circle etched into it left the imagination with a thousand and one possibilities, though a tombstone seems the most likely.

I must remember to get the post redirected when I move.

Andrew came over at three. 'Thought you were moving?' he said, helping himself to a sandwich I'd just finished making; a sandwich he would have otherwise refused if he'd known the contents.

'I will be if the agent can get his ass into gear. I should have picked the keys up on Monday, but that fell through. Hopefully it won't be much longer. I'm pissed off with this place.'

'There's a place down the road from me that's up for sale. You should make an appointment to have a look at it. I don't think it will be on the market for long!'

'Right, and where am I supposed to get the money from to pay for that? The only reason you're where you are is because some long lost relative left it to you in their will. I don't have that privilege.'

Andrew smiled, chewing on the fleshy sandwich. 'Yeah,' he said in mid chew, 'sorry, I forgot. Don't suppose you've got a beer have you?"

I handed him a bottle of Budweiser from the fridge as he finished his last mouthful of sandwich, and opened one for myself.

'Cheers mate, and thanks for the sandwich; it was great. What was in it?' I smiled. 'Sliced thigh and pickle!'

'Right!'

Friday 27th April

Alex had some girl up in the DJ console with him for most of last night; which didn't please Lloyd, who reprimanded him at the end of the session. I don't know where the woman got to; she left before I could introduce myself. Which was unfortunate! I wouldn't be surprised if she was waiting out by Alex's car while he received his dressing down from Lloyd. What she sees in the prat is anyone's guess!

The property agent's call came while I was sitting down to a bowl of cereal this morning. By ten-thirty, having listened to the agent's grovelling apologies – in other words, the other interested party pulled out – I got the keys from him.

On the way back, I popped into the bank to arrange the insurance for the Prelude. When I was told the price, I momentarily wondered if I should trade in the car and get myself a cheaper model to run. Afterwards I crossed over to the post office and wrote out a cheque to cover six months' road tax. As I was there, I also arranged to have my post redirected to my new address. I guess this weekend I will spend packing everything up, although I haven't a clue where to begin.

2 pm I'm going to die tonight! At least, I am if I'm to believe the scrawled note I found slipped beneath the door to my apartment. It didn't warrant a second look, considering the neighbourhood. I screwed it up and threw it in the bin.

Saturday 28th April

Awoke this morning and was glad to find I was still alive. My would-be assassin had apparently thought better of his intended actions.

Spent yesterday afternoon and most of the early hours, after an average evening at the club, trying to decide what was rubbish and what I was taking. Even threw out the skull of the first person I ever skinned, although I kept the jar of pickled organs. Left five bags of rubbish, and have now, at 4 pm, just about finished moving my possessions to my new home. The three bags that would have proved a threat to my freedom, had they split open when being thrown into the back of a refuse truck by the bin men, I have kept back. I will get rid of them later tonight on my way home from work.

In the rush, I'd forgotten to cancel the telephone, and had to arrange for my old line to be disconnected and for one to be installed into the new flat.

Too knackered to write anything else. I'm going out for a drink before work.

Sunday 29th April

Alex was off work yesterday evening after being involved in an accident while driving home from the club on Friday night. Unfortunately, neither he, nor the woman he was with, were badly injured; more a case of a bruised ego, although they both spent several hours down the hospital being checked out.

During the evening there was some trouble at the main bar. A customer, definitely the worse for drink, accused Lisa of stealing his wallet from the counter while he had his back turned to pass the drinks over to his colleagues. Lloyd was called, but there was little he could do other than to offer the bloke a drink on the house in a vain attempt to pacify him. Needless to say, it didn't work, and without warning the bloke laid into Lloyd with a barrage of punches. Leaping over the bar, I grabbed Lloyd's assailant and smashed him face first into the fruit machine, breaking the glass cover and giving the head door supervisor Martin and his colleagues enough time to restrain the man and hold him until the police arrived. He was fortunate that I didn't throw him out of the rear fire exit and over the stairwell to the builder's skip fifty feet below.

By the end of the night, having recovered his composure and sorely pissed that his assailant had got the better of him in front of the staff and customers alike, Lloyd has decided to take it out on me and demanded that I make an appearance in his office before work on Wednesday. I expect I'll be in for a right bollocking. Never mind, it will be worth it; there was nearly three hundred quid in the bloke's wallet. I know. I had it in my back pocket all along.

Monday 30th April

British Telecom arrived to install the telephone – surprisingly! I can still keep my old number, which makes life easier.

Tuesday 1st May

Since the death of our father, my brother and I have had little time for each other. We never got on as kids and I see little point in needless chat just for the sake of it. You can therefore imagine my surprise this morning when Carl telephoned halfway through breakfast and demanded to know why I hadn't kept in touch. Maybe I should have changed my number after all!

I told him that I'd lost my address book with his number in it, which was only a small lie, and we spoke for a while about childhood memories and more recent events in our lives, though mainly his. Finally we got to the reason for his call; to ask if I would honour him with my presence this forthcoming Bank Holiday weekend for his engagement to Elaine, his girlfriend of the past three years.

I accepted his invitation, although I'm not really sure that I want to waste my time and money on travelling all the way up to Liverpool to congratulate the stupid son of a bitch on his decision to tie himself down to one woman for the rest of his life. I'll have to think about it!

Wednesday 2nd May

As predicted, I was given a bollocking from Lloyd when I arrived for work this evening. Fortunately his temper soon abated when I convinced him that the customer had caused trouble on a previous occasion and had been abusive to the bar staff throughout Saturday night.

'It was bad enough that he should accuse Lisa of stealing his wallet,' I said, 'but for him to lay into you … that was the last straw!'

Lloyd shook his head. 'I was dealing with the situation. It did not require your intervention. If it hadn't been for you, there would have been a chance that we could have pressed charges, but as it is he's making claims of assault against the club. Fortunately for you, he can't remember who it was that assaulted him. But it looks like it will be a case of him dropping his allegations if we drop ours, and I don't like to be put in that situation. Do you understand me, Saul?'

I nodded silently. A smirk crossed my face. For a moment I thought Lloyd had noticed, as he stared up at me from behind his desk. Instead he sent me out with a reprimand.

Thursday 3rd May

Met my new neighbours from the flat upstairs earlier. A couple; both of pensionable age, and both miserable old crones. Trying to make themselves busy. They came down to complain that I had my music up too loud.

I apologised and slammed the door in their faces. Back in the sitting room I pushed the volume of the stereo up to maximum. At a guess I don't think they'll be around that long!

Saturday 5th May

A short call from Laura to let me know that she will be back home a week tomorrow at 10.30 pm.

I'll be glad to have her back. I've missed her.

Have decided to go to Liverpool; I might not get on too well with Carl but I would hate to miss a good party!

Sunday 6th May

Took the eleven thirty-five express to Liverpool. Some four hours or so later I climbed wearily from the train at Lime Street station, still regretting that, with a carriage full of passengers, I had been denied the opportunity of decapitating the Caribbean conductor who'd demanded to see my ticket at

Crewe. Bastard! He charged me for the entire journey from London. Maybe I'll be lucky next time.

In the years we've been apart, Carl hasn't changed a bit; he's still the same confident, overbearing older brother that I've always remembered him to be. And that confidence has been his key to success, aiding him up the career ladder from the position of cashier in the Whiteford branch of a well-known bank to manager of the Liverpool Smithdown Road Branch.

After a couple of drinks in a bar overlooking the docks, we drove back to Carl's; a detached house on the outskirts of the city. Carl showed me my room and apologised for Elaine not being around; her parents were holding a small family get-together for her.

Monday 7th May
May Day Bank Holiday.

Liverpool is such a friendly place! Not!

While I was walking over the waste ground alongside Parliament Street, a hulk of a man appeared from nowhere and started trying to punch my stomach out through my mouth. Admittedly this shook me somewhat. Usually I can take care of myself, and I would have had no trouble with this Neanderthal if I'd seen him coming. It wasn't until he paused for breath that I was able to take my opportunity. Grabbing him by the balls, I twisted. I didn't wait for the high-pitched squeal that was likely to find it's way through his clenched teeth. I rammed my fist up into his solar plexus. As he buckled, gasping for breath, I picked up a sharp length of wood from the ground and drove it into his chest as if he had been a vampire. Needless to say, the effect was the same. He didn't stand a chance. There was blood everywhere. As I stepped away from my adversary, he fell to his knees, then collapsed on the muddy soil, clawing at the protrusion from his body. For good measure, I raised my foot and brought it down heavily on the makeshift stake, driving it home further.

A couple of minutes later, after unconsciousness had caught up with him, I dragged his body into one of the neglected buildings; a few hard kicks at a metal support and the floor above began to give way. I exited the house pursued by a cloud of dust and debris as it collapsed in on the Neanderthal. Thank God for the party tonight; might be able to vent the remainder of my anger on another unfortunate sod.

Tuesday 8th May

Carl's engagement party went with a bang.

Returning to Carl's after the incident with the Neanderthal, I was fortunate to find the place empty, which gave me time to change out of my blood-stained clothes and freshen up.

The party started at eight, and by nine-thirty the house was packed with Carl's and Elaine's acquaintances. All night long the champagne flowed freely and, as the hours passed by, my desire for the blonde bombshell serving drinks in the kitchen heightened. The minor fact that she was Carl's fiancée made no difference at all. Toward three, when the guests had diminished to a mere handful and Carl was talking business with one of the few that had remained sober, I followed Elaine upstairs to the master bedroom.

For five minutes I waited outside the door as I listened to her undress, wander around the room and finally start the shower. Hastily I made my entrance. So fast did I move that she didn't have time to show surprise at my intrusion before I'd punched her hard in the jaw, knocking her out cold. Without wasting time, I carried her to the bed. Pulling the handkerchief from my pocket and rolling it into a ball, I stuffed it in her mouth, then secured it in place with a strip of torn sheet. When I was positive that she wouldn't be able to scream when she came to, I removed my tie and tied it around her left wrist, behind the bed head, and around her right wrist. Drawing a long, deep breath, I looked down at my future sister-in-law and stripped out of my clothes, losing a couple of buttons from my shirt in my impatience to ravish her lily-white body. Ten minutes later, with my cock drained of its juice and gripped firmly by her anal sphincter muscles, and my left hand buried to the wrist in her cunt, I heard someone coming up the stairs. I quickly withdrew, but had barely slipped on my shirt when the door opened and Carl stepped into the room. Fortunately the glass vase that he threw in my direction missed, giving me vital seconds to pummel my fist into his stomach and leave him groaning in agony, curled up on the floor.

Back in my room, I collected my things. Then I left the house, preferring a cold bench outside the station, where I am now writing this entry, to spending the remainder of the night in my brother's company.

Wednesday 9ᵗʰ May

Caught the first train out of Liverpool and arrived in London at eleven-thirty.

Back home, I found a message on the answerphone. It was Carl. Apart from calling me every name under the sun and saying that if it weren't for the fact that I was his brother he would have reported me to the police, he swore that if I ever planned on visiting either him or Elaine again, I'd be wise to take out a life insurance policy first. I don't like threats. Not even if they are provoked and come from my own flesh and blood.

Going to take a nap now. The travelling has worn me out and I've got to work tonight.

Friday 11th May

Andrew paid the club a visit, although I doubt if he remembers too much about it this morning. He and his friends were stoned out of their heads when they arrived and it wasn't long before they drew the attention of Martin and his team. Within an hour of the groups arrival, they had been escorted back to the reception area and told to leave.

Saturday 12th May

On condition that I assist with the stock-taking tomorrow morning, Lloyd has given me the evening off.

Called round on Andrew and found him slightly the worse for wear from his 'trip' last night. I was right; he couldn't remember anything about it. The last thing he could recall was leaving the Dog and Duck with his mates at closing time. How he got down to the West End, he hasn't a clue.

Laura is back tomorrow.

Sunday 13th May

I've witnessed an accident. A boy, no older than ten, ran out into the road after his football and straight into the path of a car. Mine, as it happens!

I was doing a little over sixty, and the effect was impressive. Although I know the whole thing was over in a matter of seconds, everything seemed to take place in slow motion.

The boy's legs buckled first as he made contact with the bumper and then he was lifted off his feet and spun into the air, his head impacting against the windscreen as I drove beneath him. There was a heavy thud on the roof as his body came down and then rolled off into the road. I risked a momentary glance in the mirror to make sure he was dead before hitting the accelerator in my rush to get to work on time. Fortunately no-one was around to take down the description of my car or its number-plate details.

11.45 pm Laura is late. No call from her. My only assumption is that she's been delayed somewhere.

Monday 14th May

Laura is back. She eventually arrived at seven this morning, having been delayed in Paris due to mist. I picked both her and Melanie up from the airport an hour after I received her call. Having dropped Mel off in Bethnal Green, I drove back to the flat.

After a small breakfast we went to bed. We spent the entire day in each other's arms, first in sleep and then, as the hours slipped by, making love. She has a remarkably fit body, which is now even more stunning with the golden tan she has gained while being away.

Sometime around four we got up and showered. After, while Laura searched through her luggage, I mixed up a salad.

10 pm Laura has just come off the phone, having called her parents to let them know that she is back. They suggested that she takes me to dinner with them on Wednesday. I don't much care for the idea!

Tuesday 15th May

Took Laura into the city.

First stop was the modelling agency. She had to let them know that she was back and how the trip went. As we were leaving the agency, Melanie bounded up the stairs towards us, much more lively and cheerful than yesterday morning when I'd picked the pair of them up from the airport. When I asked her why she was in such a good mood, she said that Carlos had phoned first thing this morning and asked if she would marry him! Laura then explained that Carlos was the Greek hunk that Melanie had met in Crete.

Thirty minutes later, Laura was scouring the clothes racks of Selfridges for a new dress. I stood back and let her get on with it. The latest fashion is not something that interests me. So long as a person looks and feels good, who gives a shit about what label it is!

Finally, after many more shops, we took the weight off our feet and had a drink in a small bar located off Leicester Square.

Wednesday 16th May

Dinner with Laura and her parents. It was a lovely meal but I had the strangest feeling that my presence was not entirely welcome.

Neither of Laura's parents spoke that much, and I could feel the Reverend Richardson's eyes upon me as I tucked into the beef. Afterwards, Laura took me into the front room while her parents washed up, and showed me some old photos of both her and Sabrina. Most were taken during their childhood, although there were a couple of recent ones of Laura. In some respects the girls were similar, with blue eyes and model good looks. The difference was that whereas Laura had long black hair, Sabrina's was a fiery red colour.

'Going by these, I would imagine Sabrina is a right stunner these days. I bet she has the men queuing on her doorstep,' I said, handing the pictures back to Laura.

'She's not like that. Her interests are more feminine.'

'You mean ...'

Laura nodded.

'Well I never. What a waste.'

Later, showing me to the door, Laura apologised for her parents' behaviour. 'They're a little over-protective when it comes to me,' she said. 'They always have been, but with Sabrina away I think they've got worse. Don't let them put you off me. They're harmless, just a little old-fashioned in their ways.'

Oh well, who can blame them? To have one beautiful daughter is pretty good going, but to have two, they must be over the moon! They're probably worried I'll lead Laura astray!

Sunday 20th May

Planned on spending a relaxing day with a book and a can of lager in the garden. It wasn't until I went out the back, that I realised how long it'd been since anyone had mown the lawn; the grass was nearly a foot high. Instead of the peaceful day I'd intended, I found myself getting to grips with it, first with a trimmer to cut it down in height, and then with a mower to tidy it up. Saw 'Mr Busy-Body' peering out of his first floor window as I wandered to and fro from the compost heap with the grass cuttings. He and his wife probably want to use the garden now that I've tidied it up. Well fuck him!

Laura came over later in the day after a work-out down the gym and lounged around while I finished mowing the lawn. Afterwards, when I'd done, she joined me for a stimulating session in the shower.

Monday 21st May

Found a hedgehog on my newly cut lawn. It was covered in fleas. I went to the shed and found a bottle of white spirit, then poured the contents over the animal. Within moments a ball of flame was scurrying around the garden.

Tuesday 22nd May

Introduced Laura to both Andrew and Sarah today. Fortunately they all approved of each other, though Laura was a little mystified as to what Andrew did for a living. His description of himself as a salesman did little to satisfy her curiosity. We had a couple of drinks and a bite to eat in the Dog and Duck, as ever under McCarthy's watchful eye, before playing a couple of games down the bowling alley. Inevitably I lost. Badly! Fortunately Andrew was not too far ahead of me, but of course that isn't much consolation when you are beaten by a pair of women. However, on this occasion I will let it pass.

Friday 25th May

On the news this evening they showed the aftermath of a crazed gunman going on the rampage in a small Californian hotel, killing eleven people and wounding another twelve before turning the gun on himself. I can't understand why people do that. Why on earth should they want to end it when the job is obviously only half done? By all accounts there were at least another twenty people within the immediate vicinity that he could have taken with him!

Sunday 27th May

It's still only May, but the weather is gorgeous outside. Laura joined me for a shower after having lunch with Mel up the West End, and we ended up spending the remainder of the afternoon in bed. Not that I'm complaining!

Tuesday 29th May

Someone tried to kill me last night!

I was walking back from Laura's, having seen her home after spending the evening with her in Bonaparte's, when I heard a car coming up behind me. I turned around and barely managed to avoid the vehicle, which mounted the kerb and was aimed directly at me. The headlights were on full beam, so I was unable to make out the registration details or model clearly; and as for catching a glimpse of who it was behind the steering wheel, there was no chance. I can only assume it was the same person who threatened to kill me last month.

I didn't waste my time by informing the law; this is obviously a personal matter and therefore better dealt with on a more intimate level. The only problem I foresee with this path is that I have to find out who it is that has it in for me.

Wednesday 30th May

As if to confirm my suspicions of yesterday, I received a brief phone call today from a woman:

'You won't be so lucky next time; I'll have my revenge … that I swear!'

If this had been an isolated incident I might have considered that my would-be assassin was a jilted lover from the past, but I think there's more to it than that. Glancing back over the past few months in these diary entries, everything seems to stem from around the time of Alison's death, when I received the note and newspaper cutting in the post.

I've decided to keep this matter to myself. I don't want Laura involved in something that could become a little messy.

Friday 1ˢᵗ June

Had what I suppose was another anonymous call this afternoon. The phone rang, I picked up the receiver and there was only silence. This went on a further three times, and not once did anyone speak. Tried number recall but the caller had withheld his – or her – number. I suppose it must have been the same person as on Wednesday.

Monday 4ᵗʰ June

Mel came over to see Laura and delivered the news that she has decided to accept Carlos's proposal of marriage. She's flying back to Crete as soon as possible. Laura was right; the poor girl lets her heart rule her life!

Tuesday 5ᵗʰ June

Sitting at the breakfast bar with a mug of steaming black coffee, I opened the letters: a summons for an unpaid bill to a video club – how they caught up with me I have no idea – and the telephone bill. I never realised I had made that many chatline calls this quarter. They come to nearly two hundred pounds on their own. The remaining three hundred and sixty largely covers the anonymous phone calls I make when I'm feeling bored and Laura isn't here when I get home from the club in the early hours of the morning.

Thursday 7ᵗʰ June

It's funny how you can recognise someone you've seen only once or twice, even when it's been months since you last saw them. Last night, I finally caught up with the bastard that gave me the dose of food poisoning earlier in the year.

It was nearly the end of the session and I was busy counting up the cash in my till when I happened to glance in one of the many mirrors that line the back wall of the main bar, and caught sight of him. He was a shortish man, probably no more than five-seven, in his early thirties. If I hadn't been feeling peckish at the time and considering stopping off for a kebab on the way home, he might have passed unnoticed. Unfortunately for him, it wasn't to be his night. Instantly recognising the ruffled features and receding hairline, I quickly finished cashing up the till and phoned through to reception for a doorman to escort me to the office, all the while keeping an eye on the Burger Man.

Coming out of the office, I watched him enter the gents, and followed. Inside there was only one other customer, who was just leaving. I gave the bastard enough time to lock himself in a cubicle, slip down his trousers and seat himself. Then I kicked the door in. The surprise was too great for the little cunt and he literally crapped himself. God knows what he'd been eating – probably some of his own cooking – but the shit poured out of him, filling the cubicle with an evil stench. Before his surprise could give way to the realisation of what was happening, I smacked his head against the wall of the cubicle, knocking him into unconsciousness. Hearing the main door of the toilets open, I listened and waited as a punter took a long and noisy piss, zipped up his flies, washed his hands and then left. I quickly pulled the Burger Man's trousers up from around his ankles, fastening his belt and emptying his wallet. I then grabbed his tie and made a small loop in both ends before, using the toilet seat to balance him, I lifted him up and slipped the loops over the hook on the back of the door. I peered over the top of the cubicle to make sure the room was still empty before quickly climbing over the top and dropping into the adjacent cubicle, from where I made my exit. At the end of the night, while standing behind the bar washing ashtrays, I watched the commotion as one of the door staff discovered the body still hanging in the cubicle. Although we were held back for questioning by the police, it was routine. The paramedics unofficially identified the cause of death as suicide by hanging from the moment they arrived. Naturally the coroner will have the last say on the matter, but there's really nothing to make anyone suspect otherwise. Even the smack on the back of the head could be attributed to something as simple as a fall earlier in the evening, although I will have to watch my step and not play on my own doorstep next time.

Friday 8th June

Sasha has had another argument with her boyfriend. The argument was over a girl that Sasha had seen her boyfriend discreetly – or so he obviously thought! – procure in a corner of the club.

I had been watching with amusement while he got to know the girl more intimately, when I saw Sasha walk over to the pair. Pulling her boyfriend away, she smacked him in the face with a fast left hook that even Mike Tyson would have been proud of. The next moment, her boyfriend was being hauled out of the club by Martin and another doorman and carried down the two flights of stairs before being thrown out onto the street, still declaring his innocence.

Saturday 9th June

Laura and Melanie are going to the theatre tonight. Laura was disappointed that I couldn't get the time off, but what can one do; if you don't ask, you don't get! In a way I'm doing Laura a favour. It's likely to be the last real chance that she will have of spending time with her friend. Mel's flying back to Crete on Monday.

Sunday 10th June

After work there was a party over at Leicester Park. With a couple of crates of Pils and some food that we stole from the club's kitchen, we had a wonderful time. The only thing I regretted was not gagging Sasha before I screwed her. If it wasn't for the fact that we were on the edge of the pond and that she heeded the warning I gave when I pushed her head beneath the water for a minute, I might have had the rest of the staff upon me in no time.

Monday 11th June

A great start to a new week; the sun filled the morning sky, indicating another warm day ahead. Laura came over after seeing Mel off at the airport and, walking into a junk-strewn room, decided to help me unpack the remainder of my things.

Tuesday 12th June

Laura wants to go away for a holiday. She's only been back a month and she wants to go away again. When I asked her where, she mentioned that she liked the idea of Majorca. She's never been, but has heard all about it from her sister, Sabrina, who knows some property developer out there.

Wednesday 13th June

I paid Andrew a visit. He was out with a client when I arrived, but Sarah handed me a beer and let me wait while she cut up a quarter pound bag of coke and divided it into smaller quantities for selling on to third parties. I declined her offer of a free sample. I was quite satisfied with the bottle of Budweiser she had given me.

Saturday 16th June

Andrew and Sarah were in the club yesterday evening. I wanted to speak with them, but we were too busy and I couldn't get out from behind the bar. They spent most of their time in the restaurant; one area of the club in which I have no reason to wander.

Sunday 17th June

Had an argument with Sasha over a pitifully stupid thing: the number of coat hangers, which is nothing to do with me anyway. It's the first time she has spoken to me since the party last weekend. I get the feeling that she bears a grudge, and that's not a healthy thing to do; not healthy at all.

Monday 18th June

Saw Andrew today.
'Why didn't you come over for a chat on Friday night?' he asked.
'I'm sorry. I did try, but I couldn't get out from behind the bar; it was impossible. Some of us still have to work for a living.'
We went to Bonaparte's for a couple of drinks and had a game of pool. Naturally I won. I had hoped to buy some more gear, but he's all out at the moment.

Thursday 21st June

News at the club is that Sasha has committed suicide; an overdose no less. With no alternative available, I diluted a large quantity of paracetamols in a bottle of vodka and paid her a visit Tuesday evening. Naturally, all the police found were the remains of an undoctored bottle of vodka and a few loose pills lying next to an empty container.
Lloyd asked me if I could stay behind after work tomorrow evening and help with the stock-take again. He wants to get away on Sunday, so I have to sacrifice my sleep. Mind you, the incentive of a case of beer was enough of a persuasion.

Saturday 23rd June

Finished work by six-thirty this morning and drove over to Laura's. Her parents are up north somewhere until Wednesday.

Sunday 24th June

Some bastard has stolen my fucking car. I parked it at the rear of the club as usual, but when I left at the end of the night it had gone. Vanished into thin air! I gave a statement to the police but they don't expect to find it; sixteen were stolen yesterday in less than an hour within a two-mile radius of the club. I was told not to take it personally!

Monday 25th June

Went with Laura to the travel agent's and booked a holiday to Majorca. We're going in the middle of August.

'Are you doing anything next Wednesday?' Laura asked, as we walked out of the travel agent's.

'Don't think so. Why?'

'How would you like to go to the premier of Jennifer Lopez's new film? The agency has sent some free tickets; you know, to make it more glamorous. Do you fancy it?'

'Sure.'

'Great. She's done some good films. *The Cell* was marvellous. It's one of my favourites. There's an after-show party as well, but you don't have to go to that if you don't want; those events can be a bit boring sometimes. There's only so much people can say about the film.'

'Hey,' I said, 'you know me; I'm always up for a party.'

Laura was over the moon and can't wait until next Wednesday. I didn't know she was a fan of of films such as The Cell - I guess you learn something new every day!

Tuesday 26th June

Can't go far without a car. I'll have to rely on the tube to get me to work tomorrow.

Wednesday 27th June

I found the corpse of a dead cat hung on my door this morning. No clues as to who had left it there or why.

Friday 29th June

Laura is doing a fashion show in the West End next Tuesday. She's asked me to go, but Lloyd wants me to hand out fliers with the girls, and I had to practically beg him for Wednesday night off yesterday so that I can go to the premiere. Besides, it would probably be a waste of a day. I've a feeling I would find myself spending the majority of my time in close proximity to the beer stand.

Saturday 30th June

Had a runner yesterday evening. The bastard ordered a large round of drinks from Lisa and then pissed off without paying. I saw what was going on and managed to grab the bugger before he lost himself in the crowd. Fortunately for him, when he started getting mouthy and threatened to call his mates, Martin came over to see what was happening. I told Martin all about it, and disappointingly had to hand the asshole over to him to be escorted to the exit; rather too politely, I thought.

Think I might have a chat with my favourite DJ - Alex - about the incident; I'm sure I saw his bird talking to the little shit a few minutes before he came up to the bar, and I don't think Lloyd would be too happy to hear about that.

Sunday 1st July

Had a bad night at the club last night!

My problems began when I was serving a party of assholes at the main bar. I had finished pouring their drinks and was waiting for them to decide who was paying when one cunt, a primary candidate for the nearest institution, announced that the lager I had given him was flat and he wanted a fresh one. Surprising really, when you consider that he was drinking a bottle of beer; one that I was beginning to wish I'd tampered with! Besides, he had somehow managed to force himself to drink three quarters of the bottle before deciding to complain. Naturally, I refused and demanded payment. This proved not to be in accordance with the group's liking. Not being in the mood for an argument, for once, I depressed the panic button beneath the bar, and within minutes the entire bunch of assholes were saying their farewells through the nearest fire exit. That was my first mistake of the evening! The second mistake was to turn a deaf ear to Martin when he gave me a lecture on my abusive attitude towards the customers. The moment he realised I wasn't paying him any attention, he grabbed me by the throat and pinned me against the wall, while following up his first lecture with one on ignorance.

My next mistake was to fail to heed the warning from my colleague Lisa, with whom I had arranged to share a taxi home, when she told me that the customers that had been thrown out of the club were waiting for me in the street.

To cap the evening off, my final mistake was to jump out of the taxi, while it waited for a set of lights to change, and confront the passengers of the car that had been following us since leaving the club. My chances of coming out on top against five were pretty damned small; especially when I realised that I had been set up, and that sat behind the steering wheel of the car was the cunt that had refused to pay for his drinks on Friday night. At least I managed to take two down with me. Of that I'm sure! They are lying in the beds either side of me in the hospital where I am presently committing this entry to paper.

Monday 2nd July

Lloyd paid a visit to see how I am doing.

'I've felt better,' I told him when he commented on my bruised and battered appearance.

Lloyd recommended that I not return to work until I am sure I am up for it. He's probably worried I'm going to frighten all his customers away. Fortunately , I managed to get away with only a few minor cuts and scrapes to the face.

4 pm The doctors have given me the all-clear and discharged me. I was lucky to escape with a couple of cracked ribs and bruising; more than can be said for my two room mates. One has a broken kneecap from where I jumped on his leg after decking him with a blow to the jaw, and his colleague has a cracked spinal column after I pushed him into the path of an oncoming police car. I've had a little chat with the pair of them, and they say they have learned their lesson. A little applied pressure here and there aided them in their promises to stay clear both of the club and of me in the future. Neither will be pressing charges. An interesting fact I learned from my new friends was that the motivation behind the attack was, surprisingly, nothing to do with the incidents in the club but, according to them, that some woman had told them that I had been beating up on her. That is not an action I would naturally indulge in without due cause, so who the fuck is stirring trouble for me?

9.45 pm On hearing that I'd been discharged, Laura came over with a basket of fruit and a bottle of Lucozade – her remedy for any ailment, even when inflicted by another individual. She's looking forward to the film premiere on Wednesday evening, and she's not the only one!

Tuesday 3rd July

Britain is in the midst of a heat wave.

Laura rose at six-thirty, showered and dressed in slacks and a T-shirt before having a cup of coffee and half a grapefruit for breakfast. By eight she'd left the flat and was on her way to the West End to make up for the fashion show. It slipped my mind to tell her that Lloyd had visited me in hospital yesterday and had given me time off from work. I wouldn't be content having to sit for three or four hours watching hordes of scantily clad women pass me by and not even be able to reach out and touch them. Instead, I've decided to have a wander and see where it may lead me.

Later - Ended up in the backstreets of Soho this afternoon. As I looked in the window of one of the seedier video shops, a woman approached me from behind. She rested her hand lightly on my shoulder, and I turned to face someone who thirty years ago might have been a right stunner. But the years have taken their toll.

'Would you like to come back to my place for a good time, luv?'
I gave her another look over.
'Sure,' I said, 'why not. I've nothing else to do!'
I hailed a taxi and we drove to her squat in Camden. It took me five and a half hours to peel the skin from her body; her age was not to my advantage and the wrinkles and flabs of flesh made the task at hand far more difficult than I had first anticipated. The ordeal gave me an appetite and, after checking her fridge and finding nothing, I slung a piece of thigh beneath the grill and fed off her aged, grey flesh. Arriving home around eight, I discovered a note from Laura beneath the door:

Saul,

Phoned you at work around lunchtime but your boss told me he has given you some time off. I therefore expected to see you at the show, but obviously you had something more important to do. If you can fit me in your busy schedule, maybe we could go out this evening ... will call for you at 8.30.

Love,

Laura XXXX

I'd only just managed to make it out of the shower when the doorbell rang. Letting Laura in, I quickly dressed and explained to her that on my way to the show I'd come over all faint and decided to take a detour to the hospital, hoping that I would be only a few minutes.

'Instead,' I told her, 'I was ordered to lie back and take it easy while they ran a couple of tests. They eventually told me I was suffering from a combination of sunstroke and concussion. Nothing to worry about, but unfortunately I missed the show, and I really wanted to be there for you. I didn't say anything about Lloyd giving me the time off because I wanted to surprise you!'

Laura reached out and hugged me, causing a spasm of pain in my chest from the cracked ribs.

'Oh, Saul!' she said, looking apologetically into my eyes, 'I'm sorry for doubting you!'

'Don't worry about it, it's not your fault, and I promise I will make it to your next show.'

As it happens, we decided to spend the evening indoors. Laura telephoned for a Chinese and we sat in the lounge discussing the various costumes she had worn during the day, as well as looking at the brochures the travel agent had given us when we booked our holiday. It wasn't until midnight that she announced that she had to be up early for a session down the gym and wouldn't be staying the night.

Thursday 5th July

What a fabulous evening!

Laura collected me at five-thirty and we drove into the West End. By the time we had parked and arrived at Leicester Square, the crowds were lining the barriers. Laura showed our passes and we were admitted, photographers taking our picture as we walked up the steps. Laura was used to it all, posing for a moment to give them the best view. All I wanted to do was get inside. Fifty minutes after the end of the film, we were rubbing shoulders with the likes of Jennifer Lopez, Cameron Diaz and Ben Affleck. Guy Ritchie and Madonna made an appearance, and I think I saw Nicole Kidman. Of course they weren't the only ones present, and Laura introduced me to a number of people, but by the end of the evening faces and names had become a blur and I was finally glad to get home.

Later - Phoned Lloyd and told him I will be back at work tomorrow.

Sunday 8th July

Laura's father phoned this morning. I assume he got my number from Laura. He didn't mince his words. He was blunt and to the point. He doesn't think I should see his daughter anymore.

'Why not?' I asked.

'I don't know how much, if anything, she has told you, but since the accident, Laura's been through a very traumatic period. She has been seriously ill during the past couple of years. It's only recently that we have seen an improvement in her condition, and we do not want to lose that. You seem a sensible young man. I'm sure you understand and will do what's right for her!'

'Listen Reverend,' I said in disbelief, 'I haven't a clue what you are on about and I'm sure Laura is old enough and sensible enough to make her own decisions. She doesn't need her parents to watch out for her. Christ man, we're in the twenty-first century, not the goddamned middle ages.' I think I went a little too far with the blasphemies for His Reverence, but he deserved it.

'You don't understand …'

I cut him off. 'Listen, I'm sorry to sound rude, but I'm really rather busy at the moment, so if you don't mind I'm hanging up now. I'll speak to you another time I guess.'

'No, wait …'

I hung up. I'm not having someone tell me what to do, whether it's Laura's father or not.

Monday 9th July

Laura phoned in a state of panic; her father has forbidden her from seeing me.

'I'm sorry; he went through my address book and found your number. I didn't mean for this to happen.' Laura sobbed down the telephone. 'What do we do?'

'Don't worry about it. He can't make us stop seeing each other if we don't want to,' I told her; knowing full well that the Reverend Richardson was going to try his utmost to do just that. I guess we will have to see how things work out. 'He was concerned about your health; said that you had been ill! What was this accident he mentioned?'

'Two years ago, Sabrina and I were involved in a head-on collision with another car. It was their fault. A couple with a young family – a boy and a girl, I think. Anyway, they were on their way home from a family party and he had been drinking. They were arguing, and for a brief moment he took his eyes off the road. The next I remember is waking up in hospital three days later.'

'What about the family?'

'They were fine, not even a scratch. All he got was a suspended sentence and banned from driving for twelve months.'

'And Sabrina?'

'She was waiting for me. Anyhow, for the next couple of months I had a lot on my plate, what with work and other things. Nothing more than a mild case of stress. I guess that's what my father is referring to. I'm right as rain now. You know how protective fathers can be of their daughters.'

'You were both very lucky,' I said, and promised not to do anything rash as far as her father is concerned.

9.37 pm I've just this minute put the phone down on some bitch who told me that she stole my car, took it out for a spin and managed to hit not only a cat - the one I found on my doorstep, I assume - but also a pedestrian who tried to cross the road at the wrong time. 'You may be lucky with that one,' she said. 'It was in a pretty remote area. I don't think they'll find the body for a while.' Apparently, there has also been an accident with a can of petrol, and she's dumped the car. As an afterthought, as she was about to hang up, she added: 'The worst is yet to come!'

What the fuck is going on?

Tuesday 10th July

I've painted the kitchen a violent shade of green; the cockroaches should be happy! Laura objected, but I promised that it was only the undercoat and that the end result will be well worth it. At least she seems to be in a better state since her father's little outburst. I suppose if he does find out that we are still seeing each other, she could move in with me on a permanent basis; although at times it might prove to be something of an inconvenience. I wonder if her parents know that we've booked a holiday together? It could be interesting if she hasn't told them!

Thursday 12th July

Stayed in this evening. Lloyd made a balls-up of the rota and gave me the night off without realising it. I didn't bother to tell him; I just didn't turn up for work. Spent my time brushing on the second coat of paint in the kitchen. This time a subtler olive colour.

Friday 13th July

It is often said that bad luck comes in threes, but what a day for it to happen! Laura called to say that her grandmother has had a stroke. Laura is going up to Newcastle tomorrow with her parents to visit. I offered to go too, but she felt it was better I stayed clear of her father.

A few minutes after I put the receiver down on Laura, the phone rang again. This time it was the police. They have found the Prelude; at least, what's left of it, after it having been burned to a cinder. I doubt if I'll get much from the insurance company – when they eventually decide to pay up. It's going to be ages before I get myself back on the road.

To round the morning off, I had an unexpected surprise waiting for me when I opened the second post. A court summons for non-payment of a parking fine I know nothing about. I knew there was a reason I shouldn't have contacted the DVLC when I changed my address!

When I eventually got into work, around lunchtime, I was called to Lloyd's office. He didn't look at all happy.

'Where were you last night?' He asked.

'I wasn't down to work on the rota,' I said. 'I assumed you'd given me the night off.'

Lloyd slammed his fist down on his desk and the blood in his face began to boil. Rather than antagonise him further, I offered my humble apologies and promised it wouldn't happen again.

Saturday 14th July

I managed to get the night off work again. I told Lloyd I was going to Newcastle with Laura. He didn't like the idea, but he had a couple of new bar staff starting and was more than adequately covered. I saw Laura off at eleven. We had to meet in the park a little way up from her parents' house because of her father. We then spent the afternoon painting the bedroom a subtle shade of happy violet – whatever the hell that is! Looks like purple to me. Why I let Laura choose the colour scheme I haven't a clue. I thought I might go to the cinema this evening; there's a horror double bill showing at midnight at the local Odeon: *The Texas Chainsaw Massacre* and its sequel.

Sunday 15th July

Went to the Odeon, but the painting had worn me out and I fell asleep halfway through the first film, missing the second completely.

Wednesday 18th July

Too hot to do anything more strenuous than lie in the back garden, sunbathing. Sometime around four Laura disturbed my nap, announcing her return. After a quick shower, I popped out to the off licence for a bottle of wine, while Laura put the lasagne I prepared last night, into the oven.

Thursday 19th July

The agency called for Laura. She'd given them my number in case she couldn't be reached at home. They want her to act as hostess to a group of Japanese businessmen involved in talks with a merchant bank. Her job will be to keep them occupied between the talks, which are to be held over two days next week. I objected when I first heard about it, but when Laura told me what she was being paid , in effect, for less than eight hours' work over the two days, I conceded. Even I wouldn't turn down three thousand quid for so few hours.

Saturday 21st July

God, my balls ache!

An hour and a half of pumping some little tart I picked up in the club last night was a hell of a way to spend the early hours of the morning. By six I was exhausted, and it took the last of my strength to fall out of her bed and crawl to the shower. I fortunately managed to get back to my place for seven-thirty and found Laura in a deep sleep. She needs that at the moment.

Sunday 22nd July

Awoke with the last vestiges of a dream in which I carved up Carl and threw his remains as fuel onto a fire, over which his beloved fiancée was skewered.

As I lay waiting for the images to fade, Laura awoke and complained of dizziness. It was only when I climbed out of bed that I saw the blood. For a moment I thought my imagination had crossed into the realms of reality. Instantly confusion set in, because if that had been the case then Laura would certainly not have been amongst the living this morning. The truth, as it happens, was far simpler. With the stress caused by her grandmother's illness and her father's attitude towards me, Laura's body clock had gone slightly astray and she had experienced a heavier period than usual.

After I'd changed the blood-stained sheets, taking in the rustic aroma before loading them into the washing machine, I put Laura back to bed and let her take it easy for the day.

Monday 23rd July

Went for a drink down the Dog and Duck, leaving Laura resting in bed.

When I got back at eleven-thirty, Laura was in a hysterical state. There had been another note.

you are sleeping with a murderer

Things have become a shade too personal. The problem is, I still don't have a clue who my mystery stalker is!

Wednesday 25th July

Bumped into Laura's father in Bonaparte's last night. It didn't occur to me at the time that it was some distance out of the way for him, but now I realise he must have been waiting for me. He certainly doesn't like my acquaintance with his daughter. At least that is the message he tried to put across to me in his religious sort of way. He even brought me a drink. I thought about telling him where to stick it, but to make life easier for Laura I bit my tongue and apologised for my blasphemous outburst the other day. He appeared to accept that, but then brought up the subject of the holiday. Laura had obviously told her parents. Clenching my fist beneath the table, I managed to control the explosion of fury that was building within me and calmly told the Reverend Richardson that not only would a holiday do Laura the world of good at the moment, but if he prevented her from going then he was likely to lose her. I could see he was ready to pounce with more of his religious claptrap.

'If it will make you happy, I will drop Laura when we return,' I added, 'but I will do it my way, not yours. I don't want to see her get hurt any more than is necessary!'

The Reverend mumbled something that might have been an agreement, rose from his seat and left. At that precise moment, if I'd owned a gun, I would have shot him right through his white-collared neck.

Thursday 26th July

Laura is out with her Japanese clients, showing them the sights of London and generally giving them the impression that Britain is a wonderful nation with which to do business.

Friday 27th July

I could have sworn that someone followed me from the flat this morning. Problem was, whenever I looked around, there was no-one there.

When I got to the tube station it was closed. There had been a bomb scare at Liverpool Street and all services had been suspended. Instead, I caught the bus to Bank and took the tube from there. In the process I managed to lose my shadow.

I haven't seen Laura since she left the flat this morning. I guess she's putting in some time with her Japanese clients.

Saturday 28th July

Laura can't wait until we go away. The thought of two weeks in the sun has scrambled her brains. She's only gone out and got herself a whole new wardrobe of beach wear and summer items. God knows why. It's not as if she hasn't got enough already from her modelling work.

Sunday 29th July

I was speaking to some of the other staff last night and told them that I was going away in the middle of August. Lisa thought it was great and mentioned that she's been to Majorca on several occasions. Her favourite haunts are the bars and clubs in Magaluf. She thinks we will have a wonderful time. Alex, meanwhile, made some stupid comment that no-one quite heard and went off to join his bit of stuff over at the DJ console.

I took Laura out for an evening meal at Marshal's, which appeared to have the desired effect of helping her to relax.

Tuesday 31st July

I guess it had to happen sooner or later. Last night, around nine-thirty or so, there was an untimely visit from my old friend Inspector Laws. Untimely, because when I heard the knock at the door I was in the middle of defrosting the freezer, and there were a number of items around that I would rather not have on display for the eyes of the law to glimpse. The moment I opened the door and saw Laws' sallow face, my heart sank.

'Inspector,' I said, feigning an uninterested tone. 'It's been a while. What can I do for you?'

'For a start, Roberts, you can cut the crap and tell me what this shit is about your car.'

'Sorry?' I was puzzled as to where this was going.

'The forensics have come back on that charred wreck that you reported missing. There are some interesting revelations. Revelations that would indicate involvement in a recent hit-and-run accident!'

My heart skipped a beat. Surely he wasn't referring to the kid with the football?

'I don't have a clue what you are talking about.'

'That's unfortunate then,' Laws said, grinning pathetically.

'It is? And why is that?'

'Because we're going to have plenty of time down at the station to discuss it.'

God, I could smash the smug bastard's head in with a hammer if I had one ready to hand.

'Are you arresting me?'

'If you don't want to cooperate it would be a pleasure!'

'I guess I'll cooperate, then,' I said, shaking my head in disapproval. 'But first, do you mind if I sort my freezer out? I was in the middle of defrosting it. I've got some meat I'd rather not leave out, and I'm sure you wouldn't want to pay the price if it goes off!'

'Guess not.'

I retreated into the flat and, turning the freezer back on, quickly packed everything away. I then grabbed a jacket from the back of the door and found Laws still waiting for me outside, standing next to his own car.

'This is going to be interesting,' Laws said, as he climbed into the driver's seat.

Four and a half hours, with a one hour break around midnight while Laws had to deal with some matter or other that unexpectedly came up. Four and a half hours of useless questions with Laws going round and round in circles; baiting hooks, throwing them in my direction and hoping to reel me in.

'Where's the body?'

'Whose?'

'The person you ran down.'

'I didn't run anyone down ... I've already told you, the car was stolen.'

'Was it some unfortunate drunk who stepped out into the road? You can't blame yourself ... They were drunk ... Probably better off now ...'

'Fuck off!'

'What did you do, dump the car and set fire to it in order to destroy the evidence?'

'It was stolen!'

'It's not the first time, is it?'

'What isn't?'

'That you've murdered someone. How was it with Alison Lewis? Did she tell you that she was pregnant? Was that it? I mean, that's quite a shock for any man, or wasn't the baby yours? Perhaps you had an argument and then ...'

'You're straying from the subject, Inspector. Remember! You brought me in about my car.'

'Okay, from the beginning; you reported the car stolen?'

'Yes!'

So it went on; endless questions that either I wouldn't answer or I was unable to answer. Sometime around three, and much to Laws' annoyance, I was released and permitted to make my way home. I vented some of the anger that had built up during my time at the station on some drunken youth who was staggering home from a club. A single punch to his jaw was all it took to knock him unconscious to the pavement, and a couple of kicks to his head were more than enough to finish him off, the first kick having broken his neck. I knelt beside his body and riffled through his pockets to find his wallet. There was fifteen quid still in it; enough for a taxi home. I removed the notes and dropped the wallet next to him.

Thursday 2nd August

A customer, a young man who was definitely below the twenty-one years minimum age required to enter the Ritzavoy, complained that the fruit machine wasn't paying out.

'Go fuck yourself,' I said, being the ever-hospitable barman, and continued with the job at hand; to serve the legitimate customers their drinks. If I had my way, I would rig the machines so that whenever they paid out a win the customer would get one almighty electric shock. It wouldn't be the first time that I'd done something like that!

Saturday 4th August

Had a long talk with Andrew. I think he and Sarah are going through a few problems with their relationship at the moment. Although he didn't say as much, I could tell that something was up; then again, his supplier could have let him down and he could just have been going through withdrawal symptoms at the time.

Suffered the afternoon with a headache, but have decided to go to work this evening; I'll only mope around the flat otherwise.

Sunday 5th August

Got up at two and swallowed four paracetemol straight down on an empty stomach before returning to bed for the afternoon. The headache now superseded by a full-blown migraine.

At seven, Laura phoned to remind me that in a week's time we would be setting foot in Majorca, together. She must still be having problems with her father, because she mentioned that he had expressed concern about her coming away with me. In fact everyone seems to be having problems at the moment, and they all turn to me. And to whom am I supposed to turn when I have problems? Look in the bloody mirror? Actually that's not a bad idea. At least anything I have to say will make sense!

Monday 6th August

Awoken by another phone call from the phantom bitch. This time she told me that the world was a small place. I think the poor woman is in serious need of psychiatric help.

Popped out to the bank to sort out the travellers' cheques and currency for our holiday.

Wednesday 8th August

Andrew brought Sarah into the club and I treated them to a bottle of Dom Perignon. Lloyd wasn't about and I doubt if he will miss a single bottle. I think they have resolved their differences; at least, I hope so.

The police have found the body of a woman involved in a hit-and-run accident. Needless to say, I was requested to pay another visit to the station for further rounds of interrogation from Laws. Unfortunately for him there is little he can do, since I reported the car missing prior to the woman's death.

Thursday 9th August

Went into town this morning and, while I picked up the money from the bank, Laura collected the plane tickets.

Andrew phoned to thank me for the champagne and wished me a good holiday.

Saturday 11th August

Spent the entire day repacking and double-checking everything I plan on taking, to ensure that I hadn't forgotten anything. I'd only just finished when Laura arrived laden with her own baggage.

Sunday 12th August

We're finally on our way.

It is ten-thirty in the morning and, although I managed only a couple of hours' sleep before Laura awoke me with the words 'We've overslept!', I feel on top form. Last night was uneventful, probably because I was too busy contemplating the holiday and wondering if I had forgotten to pack something, than to spend time worrying about my work. Now the waiting is over and in a short space of time we will be stepping onto Majorcan soil. In the meantime, I will relax with a glass of champagne that I have just purchased from the leggy and extremely tanned stewardess, and see what Laura can tell me of what she's learned from the travel guide as to exactly where we are staying. Someplace called Puerto Andraitx, I think!

Monday 13th August

Majorca is lovely.

We arrived to boiling hot weather, and had collected our luggage and gone through customs within twenty minutes of landing. Once outside the airport, we caught a taxi to Puerto Andraitx and to our apartment, which is situated on the cliff-face overlooking a small cove with its own sandy beach. The one bedroom apartment is small but modestly decorated, and the fridge has been fully stocked for our arrival with fresh fruit, eggs, milk, and a bottle of wine. It was a perfect start to the holiday.

After a light snack, we showered and changed into something more suitable for the Majorcan climate; shorts and T-shirt for me, while Laura slipped on a bikini top and cotton skirt. We walked the half-mile into Andraitx, wandering the narrow streets, glancing in the occasional shop window. Later we enjoyed a relaxing drink seated at a table on the quay outside one of the many bars.

It was some hours after sunset when we eventually fell laughing through the door of the apartment. Laura went straight to bed, while I put on the kettle. By the time I took her a cup of coffee, she had undressed and was lying naked on the covers. Asleep.

This morning Laura did a fry-up for breakfast. As soon as she's got dressed, I'll walk with her into town to buy enough food to last us through the next nine days. I thought we might go swimming this afternoon; the blue waters of the Mediterranean look so inviting. Perhaps this evening we might eat out at one of the local restaurants.

Tuesday 14th August

Laura mentioned that she wanted to visit the shops this afternoon. I wasn't in the mood, and I could tell she was upset when I said I would be going down to the beach instead.

Lying on the hot sand, the water lapping at my feet, I've been watching an angelic young girl, with blonde hair hanging loosely over her shoulders and dressed in her mother's T-shirt, splashing around in the water before me. I haven't seen her parents around anywhere.

Wednesday 15th August

I am sitting in bed and Laura's climbed in beside me as I put this entry to paper.

The stupid girl on the beach yesterday may have had the face of an angel, but she soon showed her true colours. It was almost an hour after I'd written my last entry and I was quietly minding my own business, relaxing in the warmth of the sun, when all of a sudden I found myself drenched with ice cold water. Rolling onto my back, I looked up to see the girl standing over me with an empty sand bucket in hand.

'Sorry,' she giggled in that pathetic manner that kids seem to have. 'It was an accident.'

Lying little brat!

On the pretence of buying her a soft drink I took her hand in mine, led her up the steps from the beach to the road and in the direction of the old town, out of sight of prying eyes.

It was just after four in the afternoon when, kneeling on the floor in the crumbling ruin of a peasant's house, I drew the knife between the child's undeveloped breasts and peeled the skin from her ribs. Right up until the end she hardly raised a hand against me. I collected a few morsels of flesh to eat on the way back to the apartment and then hung the skin from a rusty old nail in the wall, leaving the flayed body crumpled in the corner behind the door, where I unceremoniously kicked it.

Friday 17th August

Glancing through the pages of a local English paper, I came across this snippet of news:

Shack Body

The mutilated body of a murdered British schoolgirl was found in an abandoned peasant shack situated on the outskirts of Andraitx, Majorca yesterday.

Well, not to worry, I'll be going home soon.

Saturday 18th August

Asked Laura if she wanted to come out for a drink this afternoon, but she didn't feel like it. Too much sun I guess! Fortunately, she did not object to me going out on my own. Consequently I found myself seated at a bar, eyeing up prospective young women.

Unfortunately, I wasn't having much luck! The majority of the women didn't stay long enough for me to check them out; those that did were either with their boyfriends or ugly as sin. It was quite late when I discovered the one that looked a suitable candidate. She was sat beside me drinking Sangria, and didn't appear to know anyone. I watched her reflection in the bar mirror for a good ten minutes, mentally making a note of the lines along which I would run the knife; the fiery red hair that was long enough to get a good grip on if I chose to scalp her; and the manicured finger nails that could be gripped with a pair of pliers. Yes, I was pretty sure that she was the right woman, and my confidence was boosted when I realised that she had also been making use of the mirror to give me a thorough mental undressing.

70

Of the two of us, she spoke first:

'At last our destinies have crossed,' she said, throwing me entirely off guard. 'I've been waiting a long time for you.'

I was dumbstruck. Not only did she appear to be mad, but there was something vaguely familiar about her.

She watched me as she waited for a reply, taking a sip of her drink. I glanced at my watch and mentally noted that it was about time I was making my way back to the apartment. I had to act fast; if there wasn't enough time in the afternoon, what harm could it do if I arranged something for later? My reply was quick and to the point:

'Do you fuck on first dates?'

For a moment I thought I might have overdone it. The strange woman took a final mouthful of Sangria, rose from her stool and made to leave. She was about to open the door when she turned around and walked back to the bar. She asked the bartender for a pen and a piece of paper, scribbled something down and then handed the paper to me.

'Depends if you're any good!' she said; then she left.

On the paper was the address of a villa, which was located a few miles out of town, and a time, 8 pm.

Thinking about it now, she bore a striking resemblance to the woman that my old DJ pal Alex has been seeing. That's why she looked so familiar, although I can't tell for sure, because Alex's woman always tended to avoid me. Something Alex must have said, I guess.

Sunday 19th August

Arrived back at the apartment in the early hours of the morning, my shirt covered in blood from the open wound in my arm. The evening had not gone as planned.

After returning to the apartment late yesterday afternoon, I showered and then prepared something to eat for Laura.

With Laura still feeling groggy, I knew full well that she wouldn't want to go out. I told her I wanted to visit a bar over in Magaluf, which Lisa had suggested was worth checking out. By seven, I was giving the directions of my real destination to a taxi driver. Within twenty minutes, my hostess was showing me into the lounge of a two-storey villa.

I was led to the leather couch and offered a bottle of Spanish beer before being left alone. I must have drunk nearly half of it when the mysterious redhead returned. She was wearing a black, semi-transparent dress that left very little to the imagination.

'Dinner won't be ready for another hour,' she said, parting my legs and stepping between them. 'Would you like to do something else in the meantime?'

At that particular moment the thought of food was far from my mind, and I eagerly let myself be led upstairs to the bedroom.

What a mistake that turned out to be!

I'd barely stepped out of my clothes when she handcuffed my left hand to the base of the headboard. Immediately the adrenalin began pumping through my body. The thought of being at another person's disposal heightened my every sense, and the moment she plunged the knife towards my throat I was ready for her, avoiding the weapon by a cat's whisker at the crucial moment.

Grabbing the key to the handcuffs, I rolled off the bed, freed my wrist and crawled underneath.

My options, the few open to me at that precise moment, were not good. Either I could remain crouched on the floor and hope that the bitch would change her mind and leave me alone. Unlikely. Or I could get the hell out of there as rapidly as possible. I decided that the second was the more favourable of the two. Question was, how? Before I could attempt to find an answer, my attacker struck again. The blade sliced through the mattress and opened up a gash in my left arm just below the shoulder. I took my chance. Grabbing the woman's ankles, I pulled her feet out from under her. She fell awkwardly to the floor, the knife thrown from her grasp.

Slithering out from my hiding place, I made a grab for the knife. I was too slow. Out of the corner of my eye I caught sight of the woman swinging something down towards me. A moment later a chair connected with my back, and a scream left my lips with the agony. My spine felt as if it was on fire. The white specks of pain impaired my vision. As the pain faded and the room came back into focus, a hand grabbed a clump of my hair and yanked my head back, forcing me to look up into the cold blue eyes of the bitch as she stood over me.

'You're not dissimilar to me,' she said, drawing the knife beneath my chin. 'I could tell that the moment I first saw you. Unfortunately, you overstepped the line, and now it's time to pay.'

On occasions, due largely to my lifestyle, I have experienced problems with my intended victims; this one, however, was serious. Someone had seen fit to turn the tables. Instead of the redhead lying on the floor with a knife pressed firmly to her throat, it was me; and I desperately needed to gain some extra time in which to come up with a solution to my predicament.

'I don't know what you're talking about,' I said, and felt the blade press harder against my flesh; any more and it was likely to break the skin.

'Tell me, what would you do if someone you loved, Laura for instance, was murdered?' The woman's grip relaxed slightly and I shuffled my feet a little in order to get the soles of my shoes firmly on the floor. The bitch didn't notice. 'Come on; tell me. I want to know!'

I took my opportunity.

With one hand to support my weight, I rapidly drew my feet up beneath me and, from a crouching position, pushed up, bringing an elbow into contact with her groin. The effect was instantaneous. The knife fell to the floor and she let out an agonised scream. Twisting round to face her, I brought my foot up and kicked her in the stomach. It was all that was required to send her flailing through the open patio-style doors, over the narrow balcony and to her death. Stepping out onto the balcony, I looked down at the rocks below. Although there was no sign of her body, it was impossible for her to have survived such a fall. With the exception of the odd tree root protruding from the cliff face and a small ledge about twenty feet down, on which there was no sign of my adversary, there was nothing but a sheer drop of some five hundred feet to the bay below.

I turned back from the balcony and went from the bedroom into the en suite bathroom. It was there that I discovered that we hadn't been alone in the villa. Lying in the bath, naked, overweight and balding, was the corpse of a man. He was probably in his mid-forties – although it was difficult to tell, as the flesh had been peeled back and skinned from his face and his dick sliced off and left protruding from his lipless mouth. I had certainly underestimated this young woman when I first met her in the bar. After treating my wounds as best I could, I went back downstairs and, finding the kitchen, took a beer from the fridge. I then left.

Monday 20th August

Rose early to take Laura to the market in the old town. While I was dressing, Laura slipped on her way out of the shower. I quickly helped her to her feet, but she seemed to have sprained her ankle a little, and limped for the rest of the day.

The stalls in town were laden with a variety of bric-a-brac that drew Laura's attention. Every few minutes she would pick up an object that would catch her eye and ask what I thought of it, or if it would look good in the flat. By the end of the morning, we had purchased a modest collection of unusual, but useless, items that would serve as presents for people back home.

It's now been more than twenty-four hours since my encounter with the crazed woman. As far as I can tell, there has been nothing mentioned either in the press or by the locals. I can only assume that her body has still to be discovered. I've said nothing to Laura about it other than by way of explanation for the cut I received to my arm. Even then, I told her that someone had lashed out at me with a broken glass while I was in the bar at Magaluf. Although she can see that something is troubling me, Laura has remained silent.

Tuesday 21st August

Looking forward to getting back to England. Incidents such as the one I endured are best faced on home ground. Anyhow, I've one or two questions for Alex to answer. There was a marked similarity between his bit of stuff and the red-haired bitch, and it would certainly explain a few of the things that have been happening within my life over the past couple of months.

Laura wanted to know what was bothering me this morning, but how can I tell her that a woman I picked up in a bar on Saturday was a psychotic killer and came very close to adding me, of all people, to her catalogue of victims? To convince her that she was mistaken – that there was nothing wrong – I treated Laura to a meal at a restaurant in a quiet, rural village up in the mountains. After a very enjoyable evening, we took the taxi back into Andraitx and finished the night in a cosy little nightclub.

Wednesday 22nd August

Home, sweet, home.

I'm glad to be back – certainly didn't think I'd be saying that when we booked the holiday.

Start back at work tomorrow.

Thursday 23rd August

Alex has been ditched by his bit of stuff; the one with a look-a-like lying at the bottom of a cliff in Majorca. Apparently she upped and left him, stealing his entire stash of cash that he kept in an old shoebox in his dressing table. Obviously the idiot hasn't ever heard of such a thing as a bank. I asked him what her name was. His reply didn't help:

'She told me her name was Rebecca, but after she left I tried to contact her through a number of people she'd mentioned in the past, only to discover that they'd never heard of her. So, to be honest, I haven't a clue.'

Fucking plonker!

Saturday 25th August

Met the busy-body from upstairs in town. He remarked how peaceful it had been while I was away, without my music blaring up through his floorboards. He then added that he had hoped I'd left for good. I apologised for disappointing him.

Andrew came into the club earlier than usual for a Saturday evening. It looked as if he'd already put a fair amount of drink inside himself when he finally decided to tell me that he's had another argument with Sarah. This time, she's cleared out her belongings and moved back in with her parents. He wouldn't tell me what the argument was about, although having known Andrew for a good ten years, I expect it was probably something petty.

By closing time, Andrew had collapsed at one end of the bar. To anyone who didn't know that we were acquaintances, it must have looked very suspicious when I went through his pockets to find his car keys so that I could get him back home. I considered, if for only a minute, the possibility of dropping him off at his house, but I couldn't be bothered with the hassle. Instead I brought him back with me and left him lying on the sofa.

Sunday 26th August

Awoke to the sounds of retching in the bathroom. When I walked through the living room on my way to the kitchen, I half expected to see a pool of vomit on the carpet, but God had spared me such unpleasantness.

After filling Andrew with copious mugs of sweet black coffee and a couple of slices of toast, I sent him on his way. I can't be dealing with his troubles at the moment. Besides, one good fix and he won't give a monkeys about Sarah.

Monday 27th August

Now it's my turn!

Laura has gone weird on me. I don't seem to be able to convince her that I love her. Whatever I say, she manages to twist my words so that it seems that I'm not committed enough. Women! If only we could live without them; the world would be a much saner place. A little boring perhaps, but definitely saner.

Wednesday 29th August

I think Lloyd has got someone in to keep an eye on the bar staff – including me!

Throughout the evening I had the sensation that I was being watched. I couldn't tell who it was, but I was damned sure they were there. In fact the feeling was so unsettling that I didn't rip anyone off throughout the entire session.

Thursday 30th August

Woke up around eleven and, on retrieving my post, found a note written, I assume, for my attention:

you can't escape that easily

Not one of the better things to find first thing in the morning. I wish to hell I knew what it was about!

75

Saturday 1st September

Laura was mugged outside the flat in broad daylight today. The bastard who did it grabbed her purse as she climbed out of the car and then knocked her to the ground. She didn't think he was any older than sixteen, if that.

Luckily for Laura, Sabrina was paying her a visit at the time and managed to wrestle with the youth long enough to retrieve Laura's purse.

Unfortunately, Sabrina was gone by the time I got home and I was unable to offer her my thanks. I couldn't have missed her by more than ten minutes. Perhaps I'll see her on Monday; Laura is meeting her for a drink.

Sunday 2nd September

Tucked away on page seven of the *Sunday Telegraph* I found a story that had a ring of familiarity about it:

Murder Investigation

> Police are investigating the murder of British businessman and former magistrate, Tony Butler, after his mutilated corpse was found lying in the bath of his luxury villa, Andraitx, Majorca.
>
> It is believed that Butler, a timeshare property developer, had been dead for at least a week before the discovery. A female acquaintance who was on the island around the time of the murder is being sought for questioning.

Evidently they have not yet found the body of that bitch, which is a little disheartening.

Monday 3rd September

Laura met Sabrina at the Dog and Duck at eleven-thirty. I had a bit of work to do around the flat but promised to join the pair of them about twelve.

When I arrived I found Laura sat at a table on her own.

'Where's Sabrina?' I asked, sitting down beside Laura.

'Something came up at work. She had to leave,' Laura answered. 'You've barely missed her.'

'In all the time I've known you, I've never once met her. Are you sure she's not avoiding me?'

'Don't be silly. She would love to meet you. It's just that she's very busy. Sometimes I don't hear from her for months. I'm sure you will meet her soon.'

I guess Sabrina's got her reasons, but I wouldn't mind meeting her all the same.

Wednesday 5th September

Laura's received a letter from Melanie. She is still with Carlos and they have set a date for their wedding; the last Saturday in May of next year. Mel is flying back shortly for a long weekend. She wants to collect some of her belongings and see her family and friends. Laura can't wait to hear all the news.

Friday 7th September

Somebody has taken a definite dislike to me. When I got up this morning the first thing I found myself doing was scrubbing the front door step and hall carpet to remove the traces of paint that had been thrown over the door and through the letter box during the early hours of the morning. It was fortunate that Laura wasn't here because it would only have upset her. As I knelt down to clean the step, I spotted something written on the concrete in black marker pen:

b astard

I stared at the scrawled writing briefly before hastily scrubbing it off. Even then I sensed that someone was watching me, but from where, I couldn't tell. It looks as if I'm going to have to watch my back more than ever.

Saturday 8th September

Another anonymous caller. I was just getting to sleep after a hard night at work when the phone rang. When I answered it, there was only silence. I tried to check the caller's number, but – surprise, surprise – it had been withheld. When the phone rang again, I unplugged the cable from the wall socket and pulled the duvet over my head.

Sunday 9th September

Sarah called round today. She's apparently been trying to phone but was getting no answer. She came round only on the off-chance. I forgot to plug the phone back in after the calls the other night.

Sarah's visit was to tell me that it was Andrew's twenty-fifth birthday and, although they aren't together, she wanted to do something for him. She asked if Laura and I wanted to join them this evening. I guess it couldn't hurt.

I gave Laura a call in order to arrange a time for us to meet, and her father answered. Instead of slamming down the receiver on me, as I expected, he asked me to wait a moment. I heard him shouting for Laura to come to the phone. Then he came back on. He wants to see me on Wednesday, for a man-to-man talk. Weird!

Monday 10th September

God I feel ill. What a night!

Andrew and Sarah were already at the Dog and Duck when Laura and I arrived. They had grabbed a table next to the window. We only stayed for a couple of drinks before going on for an Indian.

At eleven we made our way on to Bonaparte's, and it was here that I'd arranged Andrew's surprise. A quick word with the doorman and, at eleven-thirty, the music stopped and Andrew was summoned to the DJ stand. He complied with resentment, because of the embarrassment he anticipated would follow. How right he was! The DJ quietened the crowd and, on the first note of 'Happy Birthday', played at the piano by one of the bar staff, my gift walked in.

A transvestite-o-gram. Sarah and Laura fell off their seats in fits of hysteria, while Andrew almost shit himself.

On the whole I think the evening went extremely well, with Andrew and Sarah apparently forgetting their differences. After he had calmed down and was no longer cursing me, Andrew opened a bottle of Moet and we finished the night off in style.

Wednesday 12th September

An expected visit from Laura's father, with a totally unexpected outcome.

He called at seven. Laura had gone out earlier to meet her sister. He was dressed in his usual attire of trousers, blazer and shirt with dog collar, his thinning hair wild and uncombed.

I'll never know what Laura's mother saw in him. Or, come to think of it, the church. I let him in to say what he'd obviously spent most of the day psyching himself up to say.

He announced that he wanted what was best for Laura and that, although he didn't much care for the idea, perhaps he had been a little premature in his earlier judgement of me. 'You could be just what she needs,' he said. 'But please be careful; she's more fragile than she appears.'

I was blown away. I'd never expected this of the Reverend Richardson. I offered him a drink, but he politely declined and saw himself out. Later, when I told Laura, she was over the moon and phoned her parents immediately.

Sunday 16th September

The cunt that threw the paint over my front door last week has been back again. At some point yesterday afternoon a mixture of superglue and sand was put in the door lock. I was furious. When I got into work later in the evening, Lloyd told me that there had been a phone call for me prior to my arrival. Apparently, not wanting to call back later, the woman had left a message with Lloyd. He said that the caller hoped I was coping without my car and wanted to hear all about my holiday. She would be paying me a visit as soon as possible, but for the meantime wanted to let me know she was still on the scene. When I asked Lloyd if she'd left a name, he shook his head and said no; she'd hung up without leaving it. There is only one person it could be; my anonymous caller. If that's the case, she's probably responsible for the glue and therefore the incident with the paint the other week!

Monday 17th September

Sabrina called round this evening to take Laura to an Ann Summers party. I was in the shower at the time and they slipped out before I could meet the elusive Sabrina. When I later returned from Bonaparte's, I found Laura dressed in a sexy nylon bodysuit that she'd bought.

Five minutes after I opened the door, the body-suit was lying on the bedroom floor and we were making love, really for the first time since our holiday. And about time, too. I was beginning to worry that I might have to find a new partner.

Thursday 20th September

There are occasions when life plays unfair tricks on people. Today it was my turn.

I was taking a leisurely stroll through town, when I saw a woman looking in the window of a jewellery shop. I wouldn't have paid any attention to her, or at least not as much, but I was positive that I knew her. Unable to remember where from, I passed on by. It was only as I neared the bank that I realised. She was the spitting image of the red-haired bitch in Majorca. I ran straight back to the jeweller's, but I was too late. She had gone.

Sunday 23rd September

My day did not start particularly well. In fact it would be more honest to say that it began bloody miserably! I didn't get up until eleven, when I had been supposed to meet Laura round her place at eight-thirty to take her to Windsor Safari Park. By the time I realised my mistake it was too late. The Reverend

Richardson had convinced his daughter to go with her mother instead. The deceitful bastard. When Laura eventually showed up early this evening, she apologised for going off without me, telling me that she realised how tired I was after a busy night and that Sunday was the only day I had an opportunity to have a lie in. She told me that her father had, as I'd assumed, pressurised her into going without me, and she promised she wouldn't let it happen again.

Monday 24th September

I've lost my watch. I can't find it anywhere. It's the one that Alison gave me for my birthday earlier in the year. The last time I remember seeing it was last night. I took it off and put it down on the bedside table, where I usually leave it when I climb into bed. Laura says she hasn't touched it and I've no reason to disbelieve her.

Wednesday 26th September

Took the night off yesterday. Lloyd had me rostered down, but I phoned Lisa and asked her to cover for me. It was some heavy dance night and I wasn't interested in doing it. Besides, I went to see the doctor yesterday and got him to sign me off work till the end of the week with nervous exhaustion. See what Lloyd says about that.

7 pm During a short walk beside the railway line this afternoon I found a tramp lying in a ditch.
    'Got any change guv'nor?' he slurred.
    'No.'
    'Sure right, fucking cunts all the same, the lot of you.'
    I stopped in my tracks. 'Actually,' I said, turning around, 'I may have something.' Removing a handkerchief from my pocket, I picked up an empty whisky bottle that lay on the ground beside him and that he had probably dropped in his drunken stupor. I smashed the base of the bottle against a stone. The tramp mumbled something but, before he was able to grasp what was happening, I rammed the bottle into his gut and watched with pleasure as his eyes bulged from their sockets; first in shock and then, seconds later, in pain as he tried to stem the flow of blood by plugging his finger in the neck of the bottle.

Friday 28th September

The press have caught up with my exploits. This is what I found printed inside the front cover of one of the local papers:

> A horrified couple on their way to work yesterday discovered the body of a murder victim beside a railway track near Whiteford.
>
> Metropolitan police believe that the unnamed man, thought to have been homeless, was killed in an argument over a bottle of whisky. A hunt for the killer has been launched, but a police spokesman said: 'This crime will go unsolved unless we receive help from the general public. If anyone has any information, they should contact their local police station.'
>
> The police are also trying to contact the owner of a Seiko wristwatch found in the possession of the vagrant.

I've got an uneasy feeling about the watch.

Saturday 29ᵗʰ September

Another visit from the constabulary, this time at home. God knows what the neighbours must think.

The watch worn by the tramp has been traced back to me. My name engraved on the back with Alison's was a big enough clue, not to mention my fingerprints! Fortunately they won't find my prints on the bottle.

I told the constable that I'd lost it a few weeks back, but he didn't appear too convinced. It won't be long before I have another visit from Inspector Laws. Not something I want to make a habit of. I don't like this; the police are too close for comfort. Someone is trying to set me up and I don't know who!

Monday 1ˢᵗ October

Spent the afternoon in search of a present for Laura, but to no avail. I haven't a clue as to what to get her. It's her birthday on Friday.

Wednesday 3ʳᵈ October

Thought someone was following me through town this morning, but when I slipped into a busy little bookshop opposite Bonaparte's and watched the passers-by from the window, there was no sign of my mysterious trailer. I must be getting paranoid!

Thursday 4ᵗʰ October

I've got it! The perfect gift for Laura. Walking through Piccadilly I came across an upmarket ladies' fashion boutique. I wandered in; partly because I wasn't in any particular hurry to be at work and partly out of desperation because I still hadn't brought Laura anything. Inside, an elegantly dressed, middle-aged woman greeted me. She looked me up and down with a slightly bemused expression before asking if I required assistance. Telling her I was only looking, I slipped past and began a casual, half-hearted search for something special. In a collection to the rear of the shop, I spotted a lovely ruby-coloured cocktail dress that would be perfect for Laura. I asked the shop assistant if she had one in Laura's size. She did. I paid my money and left. I wrapped the dress at home after work.

I hope she likes it! Come to think of it, I'm sure she recently mentioned that she had been looking for a new one, although as far as I can remember she has done nothing about it.

Friday 5ᵗʰ October

Laura's birthday. Gave her the dress early, before she left for work. She adores it. She confessed that she had dropped a couple of hints over the past month but hadn't known whether I'd interpreted them. The colour, ruby, was exactly what she'd been looking for, although she hadn't seen it anywhere. She's going to wear the dress this evening. I'm taking her out to Marshal's for a meal.

Tuesday 9ᵗʰ October

Found Andrew at Bonaparte's. He's had another argument with Sarah. It's time they got their acts together. One minute they're doing fine and the next they're at it like cat and dog. Stupid fools.

We played a couple of games of pool and, by the time we eventually left, Andrew was feeling better about himself. Is there another reconciliation in the making?

Thursday 11ᵗʰ October

My neighbours from upstairs were causing a commotion last night. They had the television on full volume, and even then I could hear their raised voices, although what they were saying I couldn't make out. There was the sound of breaking glass as they threw things at each other, followed by screaming. At one point I thought someone had been murdered up there! But I decided not to get involved. I've got enough things to worry about at the moment. This morning I found a note similar to the one I received at the end of August:

your time is near you bastard

I'm becoming a little perturbed by this constant assault on my privacy. If it's not anonymous phone calls, it's notes. Then there's my invisible tail. If only I knew what it was all about!

Friday 12th October

Mel flew in today.

After finding that Laura wasn't in at her parents', she called around here on the off-chance that she'd be with me. I couldn't help as I haven't seen her since Wednesday.

Sunday 14th October

Andrew invited Laura and me out for a drink tomorrow. When I told Laura, she said she wouldn't be able to make it. It's Mel's last day tomorrow and they're going someplace up the West End.

Tuesday 16th October

Had a mega night on the town last night. It took three hours and several paracetemols to bring my head down from a cyclone to a slow spin. There's only one problem: I can't remember a single thing from the moment I left Andrew and Sarah. Come to think of it, I can't remember that either!

9 pm Phoned Andrew but there was no answer.

Wednesday 17th October

Still can't get hold of Andrew. Even visited his house, but no-one was there.

Thursday 18th October

Went in to work today as usual, but my mind wasn't on the job at hand. Andrew's disappearance, although not unusual, is of some concern; especially considering that my mind is a blank when attempting to recall the events of

Monday night. In the end I asked Lloyd if I could leave early and make up the time later in the week.

Checked a couple of Andrew's usual haunts and managed to get a few words with one of his suppliers, who wasn't too pleased to hear that Andrew had done a vanishing act. 'The bastard owes me two fucking grand,' he said. I suppose there is the possibility that Andrew had done one of his moonlight flits to avoid repaying a due debt for an extra day or so, but I don't think it's likely. He's more than affluent enough to get himself out of trouble of that kind!

Friday 19th October

Heard a banging at the door and, when I opened it, found a middle aged man, dressed in a suit and tie. Not recognising him, I asked if I could help. He revealed that he was the son of the miserable old buggers upstairs and wanted to know if I'd seen them recently. I told him I hadn't, although I had heard them come and go, and their milk and papers had been taken in daily. The suited man then went on to tell me that he usually got at least one phone call a week from them, but he hadn't heard anything for a couple of weeks and was becoming concerned. I asked him if he'd tried ringing them, and he said he had but no-one ever answered. He'd even rung the police, but they'd offered little more than a 'We'll look into it when we have the manpower.' Giving the impression of the polite but concerned neighbour, I made a note of his number and promised I'd keep a look out for them and let him know if I heard anything. To be honest though, I wouldn't give them the time of day. I'm more concerned about my own friend's disappearance. There's still no news!

Saturday 20th October

I could be up Shit Street. After a tip-off from someone who saw a couple in an argument with a third person near the canal, Andrew and Sarah have been found. Dead. It's all over the television news.

Monday 22nd October

Taken in for questioning by the police Saturday evening. They picked me up at work. I was grilled for nearly five hours non-stop before I was offered so much as a cup of coffee. Once again my old friend Laws interrogated me. His persistent bombardment of useless questions ...

'Did you and the deceased have an argument at any time during the evening of their deaths?'

'No.'

'When was the last time you saw them both?'

'I can't remember ... In the pub, I think.'

'Where did you go after you left them?'

'I can't remember.'

'Were you and Miss Green having an affair?'

'Who?'

'Sarah Green.'

'Don't be fucking stupid!'

And a hundred more, all repeated time and time again. To all of which I answered the truth: I couldn't remember. Needless to say, the subject of my watch found on the tramp was also raised. I pointed out that I would be an idiot to leave my watch with the tramp after I'd murdered him, but Law's response was that he had seen people do far dafter things than that. By the time he stopped for a break, the Inspector's tolerance level had worn pretty low. I was taken to a cell, supposedly to think over the answers I'd given, but I merely wondered if Laws had finally caught up with me and, if so, where was I going to go from here.

I was left alone in the cell for another seven hours, although sleep was impossible because of the intense light and the regular banging of doors further down the corridor as the drunken bums who had also been picked up during the previous night were released on sobering up. By late afternoon, when I was taken back along the corridor to be questioned once more by Laws, I was shattered. Whether that was the intention, in a bid to break me and get me to incriminate myself,, I don't know. But it didn't work, because I had nothing to say. However hard they tried, I couldn't remember what happened on that night. I suppose they would have kept me in for questioning for as long as possible. I hadn't objected to it, as such, and no-one had actually turned round and said what they were all obviously thinking: that I was guilty. But, eventually, around ten o'clock this morning, I was escorted into a room with a video camera and made to stand in line with seven other men for an identity parade. An eyewitness to an attack on a couple near to the spot where Andrew and Sarah were found had come forward and literally saved my neck. I was released twenty minutes later on condition that I surrendered my passport to the two police officers that escorted me back to my flat. The Inspector did reveal one interesting fact: Andrew and Sarah had been found joined in a bizarre lovers' embrace. Instead of their arms being around each other, they had been placed through two open cuts situated just beneath their rib cages. An unusual fact is that Andrew was apparently missing his right hand. The autopsies are being performed at the end of the week, but death seems likely to have been caused by these wounds.

I only heard a few minutes ago, when Laura phoned to ask how I was, that the police are looking for someone of about five foot seven and slender build, with red hair. Doesn't sound much like me, thank God, but more like a woman I've met before!

Tuesday 23rd October

Mega blackout.

I awoke just after eight-thirty this morning to find myself lying on a couch at Laura's, a duvet covering my naked torso. How I got there, God only knows. The last thing I remember from last night was sitting down in front of the television at my place with a pizza, scanning through the channels to find something I hadn't seen before. According to Laura, Sabrina had apparently let me in sometime around three; Laura and her parents had been asleep in bed.

As I dressed, I realised that my shirt was splattered in blood. I had to ask Laura if I could borrow one from her father, with the excuse that mine needed a good wash. To say that her father liked the idea would be a gross overstatement. Naturally Laura offered to wash the shirt for me, but I declined. Considering I have no wounds at all of my own, I am perplexed as to where the blood came from.

Wednesday 24th October

I know what happened to Andrew's missing hand. It was in my wardrobe. I discovered it this morning when I went to get out a pair of trousers. Pinned to it and written in a not unfamiliar style was a note. It read simply:

a little gift to keep you on your toes

As to how it found its way into my possession, I haven't a clue!

Friday 26th October

Couldn't sleep much last night. I kept thinking about that last night I had together with Andrew and Sarah, but I'm still at a loss. When I did eventually get to sleep it was to be short lived. I awoke in a cold sweat. I had dreamed that I was sat in Bonaparte's with my friends when one of the bar staff came over to clear the empty glasses from in front of us. When I looked up, it was into the face of the red-haired bitch from Majorca, who was in the process of swinging a beer bottle down towards my skull. I awoke before the bottle smashed against my forehead. Scary!

Monday 29th October

In work this morning, and all I got from Lloyd, who had obviously heard of my connection with the deaths of Andrew and Sarah, was a load of questions as to what was going on. I tried to convince him everything was being sorted, but he warned that he would have no hesitation in letting me go should the club's name be jeopardised. I promised that it wouldn't be, but I don't think I can trust myself to keep any promises these days.

The funerals of Andrew and Sarah are being held on Friday. Eleven o'clock.

Wednesday 31ˢᵗ October

Somebody's been rooting through my bedroom. I found this diary lying on the floor beside the bed. When I went out this morning, it was in the bedside cabinet as usual. I questioned Laura when she got back from work, but she said she hadn't been home all day. If she had found it, I doubt she would have come home at all. But who else could it have been?

Friday 2ⁿᵈ November

The funerals of Andrew and Sarah were held simultaneously at the crematorium. Their coffins lay side by side on metal roll bars, to the left of the priest.

The service was a simple affair. It was attended by some thirty people, mainly family, although as well as Laura and me there were a couple of other friends and a few of Andrew's business clients. As the coffins rolled slowly through the blue curtain, a woman seated in the front row – I later discovered it was Sarah's mother – broke down in tears.

Afterwards, as the mourners congregated outside to look at the display of wreaths, Laura and I slipped away at my request and came back home.

Sunday 4ᵗʰ November

Had lunch at the Dog and Duck on my own. Laura had another celebrity bash to attend last night and didn't want to disturb me when she came in, so she went back to her parents' place. After seven pints I still felt sober. I remain at a loss about Andrew and Sarah. I can't understand how it happened.

Monday 5ᵗʰ November

My brother Carl is dead!

Laura broke the news to me at dinner. Elaine phoned while I was in town. Apparently he interrupted a burglar in the early hours of Sunday morning. He died of a single stab wound to the chest. Elaine was in bed asleep at the time. I'm not sure how I'm supposed to feel. It's certainly one funeral I won't be bothering with. I guess I should go out for a drink and celebrate.

Sunday 11th November

Typical; of all the places she could want to go, Laura asked me to take her to church. Her grandmother died in the early hours. There is little anyone can say at a time like this so I obliged, enduring the hour-long service. I even put some money in the collection dish, although I don't think she noticed. The funeral will be some time within the next two weeks. I'll have to ask Lloyd for another couple of days off from work, which I doubt he will like.

Monday 12th November

Laura has returned home to comfort her mother. They are both going up to Newcastle on Wednesday to help sort out her grandmother's affairs. The funeral will be held on the twenty-first.

Tuesday 13th November

Wandering around the flat today I got the impression that someone had been in here while I was down the pub. Little things like a glass on the draining board and a bottle of Beaujolais, which I'd had a couple of glasses from before I left, but then put back in the cupboard under the sink, not on the unit beside the oven. The other thing I noticed was that the sliding doors that open onto the patio were slightly ajar. I know that I checked them before I left. After I locked them, I put the key on the coffee table. Now it's back in the lock. Someone must have opened the doors from inside and gone into the garden, and on coming back in failed to slide the doors shut. But who, and how did they get in? Laura and I have the only keys! And, from what I can see, nothing has been stolen.

Wednesday 14th November

Laura has gone. I know how much her grandmother meant to her. It's such a shame when one considers how she managed to pull through to an almost complete recovery after her stroke in July. But as they say, when your time is up, it's over. You might be able to borrow a little longer, but eventually the grim reaper will whisk you away. I'll have to phone Laura later to see if she's arrived safely.

Thursday 15th November

Spoke to Laura on her mobile. She's arrived okay and suggested that I come up to the funeral next week. Not an idea I like the sound of, considering I'm not even planning on going to my own brother's funeral, so we will have to see.

After work I went over to Moody Blues with Martin, where we remained until eight this morning drinking a varied combination of watered-down spirits. I should sell them some of the concoctions I use in the club; they would soon liven up their business! 'Drinks guaranteed to knock you out; beer to send you over the edge.'

Went straight back to work in the morning, without having come home to change first, which resulted in a further round of questions from Lloyd. Anyway, I've showered now and changed into a clean shirt and trousers for work tonight. Tomorrow I don't have to go into work until early evening, since Lloyd will be at an out of town meeting and he's going to give me the keys to open up.

Friday 16th November

Woke up fresh and fit enough to take on the world, but now, after a couple of hours, having eaten breakfast, I feel lethargic. I think I'll pop down to the shops for a pick-me-up.

Sunday 18th November

Exhausted. Awoke around six this morning and found myself lying beneath a bench in the park. My clothes were torn and covered in blood. And my head ached like hell.

The last thing I remember is walking out of the house on Friday. What is happening to me? I've got to be losing it. There's no other explanation. God only knows what Lloyd is going to say.

Monday 19th November

I've been sacked. What else could I expect? Lloyd was furious. More than I've ever seen before. But then, I suppose he had every right to be. Apparently he hadn't returned from his meeting until after eleven, by which time the Ritzavoy staff, having waited for over two hours, had buggered off elsewhere and made the most of what was left of their unexpected night off. Lloyd kindly calculated, for my benefit, that the Ritzavoy had lost in the region of fifteen grand on Friday, and probably a proportion of its customers. He booted me out of his office without so much as a thank-you for my service.

Things seem to have gone from bad to absolutely terrible over the past couple of months. When will it all end?

Tuesday 20th November

Found this in the paper this morning:

Parents return to bloodbath

Mr Peter Sunderlin and wife Mary returned to their home in Whiteford at around 11 pm on Saturday, having spent an evening at the theatre, to discover that their two children, Amy (4) and Simon (6), and the babysitter, a Miss Nicole Hunter (18), had been brutally slain and set alight. The police are unwilling to comment on the incident, but it is believed that there is a link with a number of earlier unsolved crimes within the local area.

I don't like the look of it. I'm not saying for a moment that I did this, but considering the fact I haven't a clue what I did over the weekend, I'm hardly in a position to convince anyone else otherwise! As for the link to earlier unsolved crimes within the local area, considering the events of the past few months, this is all beginning to look just a little too coincidental!

Wednesday 21st November

Caught the train up to Newcastle, and Laura met me at the station. She drove us back to the house, where the relatives had begun to assemble. While Laura made herself busy serving coffee and greeting Aunts and Uncles she hadn't seen since she was a child, I sat in silence, collecting my own thoughts on what I was going to do without a job.

My third funeral of the year was what one would expect for that of a popular spinster with a vicar as a son-in-law. Five cars of close relatives and a good sixty or so friends were waiting for us at the church.

I decided against mentioning to Laura that I'd got the sack, at least for the time being. She already has enough on her hands without the addition of my own personal problems. Instead I played the perfect gentleman/boyfriend, much to her father's dismay I hasten to add, and gave Laura the comfort and support she required to get her through the day.

Later, her mother thanked me for being there for Laura, in particular for this last week or so. Under the circumstances I decided not to correct her on the fact that for the past week Laura has been with her in Newcastle.

After she had helped her mother clear up the house, an hour or so after the last relative had departed, Laura asked if I minded returning back home tonight. The funeral had obviously been too much and she wanted to get back to familiar surroundings as quickly as possible. The journey back was made in silence. Laura, lost in her thoughts, stared out of the window while I drove her car.

I was surprised Sabrina hadn't been at the funeral. I'd said as much to Laura's father, but he'd just glared at me as if I was a piece of shit on the sole of his shoe! When I mentioned it later to Laura she said that Sabrina hadn't been able to make it. She didn't explain her father's reaction when I'd mentioned her sister's name.

Tuesday 27th November

It was revealed in the evening paper today that the weapon used in the murders last week of the Sunderlin children and their babysitter was the same instrument that had been used in the murders of Andrew and Sarah, as well as in a couple of incidents earlier in the year.

As soon as I read the article I went straight into the bedroom and checked the wardrobe. There on the shelf, exactly where I'd left it, was old man Finney's knife. So why then do I still feel uneasy about this latest revelation?

Thursday 29th November

Laura went out on a photography shoot at a studio in Kensington. Sabrina is meeting her for lunch. I suggested catching up with them as well, but Laura told me not to bother. I don't think she wants me around. Instead, I decided to go down the Dog and Duck, where I chatted up a busty and moderately good-looking barmaid named Karen.

After she finished her session I walked her home. Unfortunately for me, though luckily for her, her boyfriend had taken it upon himself to phone in sick today of all days, and I beat a hasty retreat.

Friday 30th November

Found some photographs of Andrew and me taken a few years back during a day trip to France to stock up on some much needed supplies of alcohol. Andrew's and Sarah's deaths still have me at a loss. If it wasn't for the eyewitness, I would be locked up by now! I am unable to piece together the small remnants of memory that I have of either that evening or the weekend of the deaths of the Sunderlin kids. Furthermore, what of the blackouts that I appear to have suffered around the times of both those events? How are they connected?

Saturday 1st December

Laura and I have had an argument. She stormed out of the flat about two hours ago.

'You're an inconsiderate bastard,' were her parting words.

Why? I haven't a clue.

I lost my temper with her then and slapped her across the face; not hard, but enough to break her pride. I didn't do it intentionally; I couldn't control myself. If only she knew what I'm going through at the moment.

Sunday 2nd December

She's back!

Laura crept in a few minutes after I finished yesterday's entry. I apologised to her but she told me to leave it. As far as she's concerned the matter is closed. But it isn't. If only I could find a way of explaining how I feel at the moment. I don't want to hurt her; I love her too much for that.

Monday 3rd December

Another nightmare last night. This time I was reliving my experience with the red haired bitch from Majorca making an attempt on my life. I managed to wrestle her to the floor before fixing my hands firmly around her neck.

The images came to an abrupt end when I was awakened a little after five by screaming. It was Laura. My hands were gripped around her throat. For the remainder of the night Laura sat at the kitchen table staring into a steadily cooling mug of coffee.

When I rose around eleven she was lying on the table, head in arms, asleep. The tears she'd been crying had dried on her cheeks, and her coffee was half drunk. I carried her effortlessly to the bedroom and lay her on the bed, covering her with the duvet so that she might get some proper sleep.

Tuesday 4th December

The sleep seems to have done Laura some good. She hasn't mentioned my attempt on her life. Perhaps she thinks it was part of her imagination; that she'd been dreaming it. If only that was true!

If things continue in the direction they've been going these past couple of months, I fear that I will go crazy. Christ, some people would say that I already am!

Wednesday 5th December

Laura has gone. She moved out yesterday, taking what few belongings she had here with her; even her toothbrush. I'd only popped into town for some odds and ends. I couldn't have been gone for more than fifteen minutes. Yet when I returned, she'd gone. The only evidence that she'd been there at all was a note I found, beneath the sugar bowl, on the kitchen table. It was written in her hand.

> Saul,
>
> I need time to think. It's not every day that your boyfriend tries to strangle you in your sleep. Sabrina suggested that I go to the police. I think she's wrong, but I need time to think things through.
>
> Hope you understand and please don't try to contact me.
>
> Laura.

What right did Sabrina have telling Laura to phone the police?

Thursday 6th December

Called Laura's place and her father answered. Recognising my voice, he told me that Laura didn't want anything more to do with me. Then he cut me off. Rang back a couple more times but the number was engaged. He must have taken the receiver off the hook.

Friday 7th December

Wandered past Andrew's last night, on the way back from Bonaparte's. An estate agent's 'For Sale' sign has been put up in the garden within the past week.

Saturday 8th December

Another note, more detailed than the others:

93

ive been with you through thick and thin and now it's time to make you pay for your biggest sin that night you prayed that the bitch had died

This time the note is written in what appears to be blood.

Sunday 9th December

2 am I can't get to sleep through thinking about that blasted note. A few minutes ago the phone rang. When I answered it there was silence, the same as on previous occasions. I'd just got back into bed when it rang again. This time when I answered it, a voice – a woman's voice, though not Laura's – whispered: 'I'm going to have your balls on my table for breakfast ...'

Since I can't get to sleep and I've got it in my hands, I think I might read through this diary. There must be something somewhere.

11 am The voice; the notes; the recent murders; even my dreams. They're all here in my diary, and I've barely given them a second thought. Until now, that is!

In some way or another, they are all connected. Exactly how, I'm uncertain. The answer is probably staring me right in the face, but I can't find it. One thing's for sure: I need to find Laura, because she could well be in danger.

Monday 10th December

Went round to Laura's house and confronted her father at the door. I attempted to explain as rationally as possible that it was imperative that I spoke to Laura. The Reverend's answer was: 'No; she's not here.'

'Well, can you tell me where I can find Sabrina?'

His reaction at the mention of his second daughter's name was even more extreme than at the funeral..

'How dare you! You come into my house, you upset Laura, and then ... then you have the audacity to pour salt on wounds that have only just begun to heal, by bringing Sabrina into this. How dare you.'

'Listen, I don't know what your problem is, but if you just tell me where Sabrina is, I'll ...'

'Leave us alone. I warned you that this would happen. Now leave us before you make matters worse.'

The door slammed in my face, leaving me stunned by the outburst from the priest, and well and truly pissed off. Once I've sorted things out with

Laura I will be paying the Reverend a visit, and he won't be slamming doors in my face again. Far from it.

Tuesday 11th December

Got a phone call from Mr Huttle, the son of the upstairs couple. He asked if there had been any sign of them. To be honest, I'd forgotten all about our last meeting. I asked him to give me a couple of days and then I'd get back to him. Went around to Laura's. Her mother answered this time. I told her I had to see Laura immediately. She looked at me and shook her head, said she wasn't home, she hadn't been home all night, she'd gone out yesterday evening and hadn't returned.

What can I do now? Wait until Laura shows up again – if she does – or try and find her? To do that I need to find Sabrina, and I don't have the first clue as to where I should start.

11.20 pm Returning from the Dog and Duck, having gone on the off-chance that I might find Laura there, I saw a light on in the upstairs flat. I knocked on the door but there was no answer. I left it at that. They could have popped out and left a light on for security.

Wednesday 12th December

Phoned Laura's and was told that she still wasn't back.

Went out to get a paper, and when I returned I noticed that the milk had been taken in for upstairs. I banged on the door again, but no luck. After I'd been in the flat for a couple of minutes I heard the door to upstairs open and close as someone left.

Why can't they be bothered to answer my knock? I'm only trying to do them a favour.

Thursday 13th December

If my suspicions are correct, I have a good idea where my adversary is hiding herself. There's something I need to check first, and then I will know for sure

Phoned the number that Mr Huttle gave me and got the switchboard for a company of solicitors based in the city. After a moment of listening to a computerised version of Beethoven's fifth symphony, I was put through to my neighbours' son.

'Have you heard from your parents yet?' I asked.

His answer was as I expected: 'No!'

I told him to be patient and that I might have some news for him shortly, then hung up.

It's nearly midnight. I heard someone go upstairs about half an hour ago. As soon as they got in I switched the hi-fi on and turned it up to full volume. I haven't heard so much as a thump on the floor. Rather strange when you consider their previous reactions when I had my music on at even half volume.

I'll have to wait until the right moment before I can prove my theory correct, but I think Mr Huttle's parents are both dead and probably have been for as long as two months!

Friday 14th December

I don't know where to begin. My mind is still reeling from the revelations of the past few hours. But with hardly any sleep last night – short naps more than anything, while waiting and listening – if I don't get everything down on paper now, I doubt if I ever will!

It was around seven this morning when I left the flat and forced the lock to my neighbours' door upstairs. Inside the hall the familiar odour of death was heavy, and my senses were instantly alert.

Creeping stealthily up the stairs, I paused at the landing and did a quick check of my surroundings. To my left was the kitchen and bathroom, their doors open, no-one inside. Adjacent to the bathroom, and almost opposite from where I stood, was another door, this one closed. And the same with the door to my right.

I decided to take the door opposite first. I opened it slowly, and the putrefying air rushed into my nostrils. The room was in darkness; the curtains had been drawn. Running my hand over the wall, I found the light switch and flicked it on. There before me were my neighbours.

Their chewed, mutilated corpses lay on the bed, probably in exactly the same position as the day their throats had been slit open.

I took a hasty look around the room and a quick glimpse beneath the bed, but there was nothing else to be found there. I crept out and pulled the door shut behind me. Having already seen that the kitchen and bathroom were both empty, I was left with one room to check; the sitting room. I opened the door and turned on the light.

There, hanging over the back of the sofa, was Laura. She was naked and appeared to be both bound and gagged. Strips of flesh hung from her breasts; both nipples had been sliced off. One I could see clinging to the edge of the bowl that had been placed beneath her to collect the blood that dripped freely from her wounds. It looked as if she was dead.

I stepped forwards for a closer look and, as I bent down to remove a strand of blood-soaked hair from her face, her eyes flickered open. The dull glaze of pain could be seen deep within.

I could see a tortured look of relief when she recognised my face, but it was short-lived. As I was removing the gag, her expression swiftly changed into one of hatred. It was enough of a warning for me to dive to the floor as a blade cut through the air above me. The ropes that had apparently bound her fell to her feet as she rose from her former position. As I rolled away, something on the coffee table caught my eye. It was a hairpiece. A hairpiece of long, red hair. It was then that I realised that the woman now standing before me with hatred burning deep in her eyes was not the Laura I knew, but the red-haired bitch from Majorca. They were one and the same. The how and why were to come, but what mattered for the moment was that she was waiting for me to make a move, and in her hand was a knife. A knife I recognised as the one I had once wrestled from a pensioner's grasp when he'd turned on me at the cash machine. The knife that should have been on the top shelf of my wardrobe.

Unlike that time in Majorca, on this occasion I was prepared. But I had not anticipated the scene I was now in, and I really didn't understand what was going on. 'Why?' I asked, cautiously rising to my feet.

Laura looked at me, scratching at her chin with the knife, pondering her answer. 'You really don't know, do you?'

She was right; I had no idea.

'You stole the one person I loved, and then you *brutally murdered her*.' She practically spat the last three words. It was here that my mind was having difficulty in getting to grips with what she was saying. One might say that there have been more than a few people who have come to an untimely end having crossed my path, but never before have I experienced a problem such as this as a result. Laura must have caught the expression on my face. 'Alison, you bastard!' she erupted venomously. 'It was Alison Lewis, your ex-girlfriend! I was begging her to return to me that night, but no, she loved you; you were the father of her unborn child and she wanted to try to make a go of it. Yet you didn't want to know!'

'But Laura …' I managed to stammer, while keeping my eye on the knife. This made her laugh.

'Laura! That loser. I'm Sabrina, you pathetic prat!'

Reality finally dawned. How could I have been so naive? I should have known better. All the time, I had thought that Alison's ex had been another man. Never had I considered the notion that it might have been a woman. No wonder Alison had been so certain that I was the baby's father. It was Sabrina she had been arguing with on that fateful night. Sabrina who had watched Alison run after me before I plunged the knife into her. All my troubles stemmed from that period, and Sabrina had even been at the funeral; the veiled woman. How fucking stupid could I have been? At least I now knew why.

'That brain of yours must be working on overtime.' She said; a smile spreading across her face. 'Are the pieces of the jigsaw beginning to fit into place yet? It doesn't look like it from where I'm standing. You can't understand what's happened to your precious Laura can you… She's right here. Don't you recognise your own girlfriend when you see her?'

It hit me! I remembered something that Laura had said in the past, when I'd asked her about the accident that her father had mentioned to me.

'The accident …,' I started. 'When Laura was in a coma for three days afterwards. The head-on collision. Laura was the only survivor, wasn't she?'

'Is that what you think?' Sabrina glared at me. 'No, she wasn't the only survivor. The family in the other car, they survived. Though they didn't deserve to. He was well over the limit, and it was his wife, with her moaning, who caused him to take his eyes of the road. What did he get? Nothing but a slap on the wrist and a meaningless fine imposed by some short-sighted magistrate. They've paid for it now though. All of them. I've made certain of that. The same as your beloved Laura is paying for it now. Just imagine, every time you made love to Laura you were really fucking me. You don't know how much I detested it. It was nauseating.

While I watched, Sabrina looked down at her body – at Laura's body – and flicked a strand of loose flesh with the knife. I could now see that the blood and gore had been applied, and that Sabrina, having anticipated my visit, was, in fact, uninjured. The effect had been purely for my benefit. 'Laura was weak. Even when we were children, she was the mouse and I was always looked upon to care for her. When she came out of the coma she took it badly. They all thought I was dead, you see; and weak little Laura, she blamed herself for my death. She was in and out of hospital for months after the accident, suffering from depression. All the time I kept my distance, maintaining a low profile until the doctors said that Laura was no longer a danger to herself. She made quite a good recovery, don't you think?'

A cut appeared above her waist as Sabrina drew the knife lightly across her own flesh. She then raised the knife to her mouth and licked the fresh blood from its blade.

I was running out of time.

'She returned to work and pretty much led a normal life. But all the while, I plotted my revenge, taking over Laura's body for my own use whenever I felt the need. On one such occasion I met Alison, and we became lovers. But it wasn't to last. Laura was partly to blame. She wasn't too keen on the relationship. It wasn't her thing! Alison also had reservations of her own at the time … then she met you! Did you know that I followed the pair of you into the park that night? I heard Alison cry out, and when I got there, you were kneeling over her body. I waited until you left before seeing if there was anything I could do for her, but it was too late. She was already dead!'

The revelations had taken me by surprise, but now I realised that I needed to take control of the situation as quickly as possible.

Sabrina continued: 'At that very moment, I swore that I would make you pay for taking Alison from me, and decided that I would wait for the perfect opportunity. That opportunity, I thought, was in Majorca. I was obviously wrong. I expect you thought I was dead. I remember your face when you got back to the apartment that night, hoping that Laura wouldn't notice that something was amiss. If you'd only known that I'd barely managed to make it back minutes before you!

'How? There was no way you could have survived that fall; it was over five hundred feet!'

'You're right,' Sabrina smiled. 'there was no way I could have survived that. If it hadn't been for a fortuitously placed tree root in the cliff-face, I doubt if we would be having this conversation now. I managed to swing myself onto a small ledge. There was a narrow crevice in the cliff, barely big enough for me to hide in, but it was enough to keep me from your sight. The biggest problem was climbing back up the cliff-face; that cost Laura a couple of well-manicured nails. As it was, I was lucky to escape with barely a scratch – just a sprained ankle – although I was wondering how Laura was going to explain that one to you. Fortunately, an opportunity arose for her to "slip" on the way out of the shower the next morning.'

I glared at Sabrina. For months I had been taken in by her. If only I hadn't been so short-sighted.

'After you returned to England, I promised myself that I would have my revenge, not only for Alison's death, but also for the humiliation you'd caused me. No-one has ever escaped their demise from my hand – until you, that is! When Laura was in bed with you, I often watched while you slept, and thought how easy it would be to slit your throat there and then. As you can tell, I resisted the temptation. There were times when I came close to the edge, but I wanted to make sure that you suffered as much as I had; that you lost everyone that was close to you.

'Andrew and Sarah!'

She was enjoying this. 'Once I'd slipped you a dose of a little home-made sedative – a combination of barbituric acid and coke – it was easy. You blacked out for ages and I was free to come, go and do as I pleased. Which hasn't made it too difficult to set you up to take the blame. In fact, I've had some interesting conversations with a friend of yours; a man by the name of Inspector Laws. He's quite keen to see you behind bars. It seems he has an entire filing cabinet dedicated to you.

I thought I might be seeing you today. After all, it didn't need a genius to work out where I was. I'd wondered if dear old Dad might give the game away, but he likes to remain tight-lipped where I'm concerned. Anyway, I gave Laws a call ... you know ... to cover my back ... just in case. Unfortunately all I could get was his answer-phone ... not what I'd been hoping for.'

I was fuming. The bitch had been setting me up for months and I hadn't realised.

'It wasn't all bad, I guess.' I needed to distract her. 'I bet you never thought you would do me a favour, did you?'

'I beg your pardon!'

'Well, I assume you were responsible for murdering my brother. After all, Laura wasn't with me that night, and it's not that difficult to do a round trip to Liverpool in eight hours or so.'

Sabrina smiled. 'Yes, you're right. Unfortunately he didn't know what hit him. I had hoped to make his death a slow one, but we can't always have it our own way.'

'You're right. What you didn't know was that my brother and I didn't get on at all well. In fact, to say that he hated the very thought of me would probably be an understatement. So, to be honest, you did me a favour and saved me the expense of going up there and doing the job myself.'

'You bastard!'

As Sabrina ran at me with the knife, I bent down and grabbed hold of the loose end of steel chain that hung the length of my leg inside my trousers. I pulled, and the other end, taped to my thigh, came free. I whipped the chain out, stepping forwards as I did so, and it found its mark, wrapping itself around Sabrina's wrist. I jerked it back and the knife flew towards me. I ducked to one side, taking Sabrina with me. The knife hit the floor. I pulled Sabrina towards me and wrapped the chain around her throat. This time I was going to make certain that I did the job properly! I pulled the chain tight.

'Saul, please!' It was Laura's voice. 'Please don't.'

I looked at her face; there was no-one there but Sabrina. But in the moment of my hesitation, Sabrina lashed out and caught me a glancing blow to the head. I reeled as the woman struggled free of the chain and dived for the knife on the floor behind me. I flicked out with the chain and caught her legs. She hit the floor hard. Her body was now motionless.

Breathless from the sudden bout of exertion, I got to my knees.

'Sabrina?'

No reply.

'Laura?'

It was then that I noticed a dark pool of liquid spreading out from beneath her. I pushed at the body with my foot, and it keeled over to one side. To her credit, Sabrina had managed to reach the knife – although little good it had done her when she had fallen upon the blade, the handle of which was now protruding from her chest. She was dead. I had been cheated of my own revenge.

If the truth be known, I think Laura died some time ago, and Sabrina has been using her persona as a mask.

I dropped the chain and pressed my fingers to her throat, feeling for a pulse. Nothing.

I felt empty inside. Absently I dipped my finger in the blood coming from the knife wound and touched it to my tongue. Sweet.

I've written all I can here. Now I need to sleep.

Saturday 15th December

11.23 am All hell has broken loose outside! I don't think it's going to do me much good trying to explain what happened upstairs. It looks like someone has already jumped to conclusions. I knew I should have left immediately, but the temptation of the body and the lack of sleep finally caught up with me. It looks now as if I've left it too late! There are armed police running around all over the place. I've seen two marksmen in the house across the road; one upstairs and one downstairs. Riot vans are parked at either end of the street, blocking out civilian traffic.

Someone is speaking through a megaphone. I think it's my good friend Inspector Laws. The bastard! It looks like he got Sabrina's message after all. He wants me to leave the building with my hands in the air where they can be seen. He's been watching too many movies, I think! What the hell does he think I'm going to do; go running out with a machine gun or something? Sure. I wish. Maybe I wouldn't be so concerned then. Unfortunately, I don't own a gun of any kind, and I would be a fool to think that I could take on the numbers they've got out there, on my own.

Considering the current circumstances I don't think it would be a wise idea to leave this diary lying around for any old soul to pick up after I've gone out there. The last thing I want to do is make the life of an asshole like Laws easy by leaving him a load of incriminating evidence. I think I'm going to...

Thursday 20th December

'Psycho' Charged

Saul Roberts, 26, of Newton Road, Whiteford, E19, made a brief appearance at the Old Bailey today, where he was formally charged with eight brutal murders. The victims were his neighbours, George and Eileen Huttle, his former girlfriend, Laura Richardson and, in crimes dating back to last October and November, his friend Andrew Chase, and Chase's girlfriend Sarah Green, siblings Amy Sunderlin (4) and Simon Sunderlin (6) and their babysitter Nicole Hunter. It is expected that further indictments will follow.

Roberts spoke only to confirm his name and address. An application for bail was refused.

Dr Robert Wilson
Stonehouse Road Surgery,
Stonehouse Road
Whiteford
London E19 9DZ

28th December

Dear Inspector Laws

Forgive me for not contacting you sooner, but I have only recently been informed that one of the victims in the Saul Roberts murders was a former patient of mine. I recognise the high profile of the case, but there are a number of points to which I should draw your attention with regard to Miss Laura Richardson.

Laura came to me approximately two years ago suffering from what appeared on first diagnosis to be a form of depression. This was after she and her sister Sabrina (who was two years her senior at the time) were involved in a head-on car crash, as a result of which Sabrina was critically injured and later died in hospital. From my own knowledge of the family, the two sisters were very close; and, as the older of the two, Sabrina always looked out for Laura. Of course, Laura blamed herself for her sister's death and became withdrawn. That was a normal reaction under the circumstances. However, in Laura's case, something snapped. She couldn't accept that her sister was dead. In fact, in her mind, Sabrina was still very much alive – so much so that she developed a split personality. On the one hand she was still Laura, the face that everyone knew, but on the other hand she was also Sabrina, still keeping a sisterly watch over Laura and taking control whenever she felt that Laura couldn't handle the situation. The two personalities were very different from each other, right down to having their own individual styles of handwriting. Although they shared a single body, the Sabrina persona made every effort to make herself unrecognisable from Laura. Once the schizophrenia was identified, it was possible to control it with treatment, and within six months Laura was able to return to a relatively normal life, while she continued with her medication.

Unfortunately, Laura's regular visits to me and to her psychiatrist eventually ceased. I spoke at length with her parents, who were of the opinion that Laura was cured. I was sceptical about this, as experience demonstrates that patients such as Laura require treatment for a much longer period of time than was the case here.

No doubt you are wondering why I am writing to tell you of this, and what the connection is to the case in which you are currently involved. I have recently read that Mr Roberts has been charged with the murders of the Sunderlin children. I know that this may be a coincidence, but I have double-checked my notes to ensure that I am not mistaken. The driver of the other car involved in the accident in which Sabrina died was a Mr Peter Sunderlin. Obviously I am unable to come to any informed opinion on the circumstances of the Roberts case, but if there is indeed more than a coincidence here, I hope that this information will be of some assistance. Please feel free to contact me if you have any queries.

Yours sincerely

R. Wilson

Dr Robert Wilson

About the Author

With a career in the bar and nightclub scene behind him and currently employed in IT within local government, Alistair Langston has previously written lyrics for the stage musical *The Beast in the Tower* in addition to the short musical film *Glamour Overdrive*. He currently lives near Glasgow, Scotland where he has a number of projects in development. *Aspects of a Psychopath* is his first novella.

Visit *Aspects of a Psychopath* online: http://www.aoap.co.uk

Also available from Telos Publishing

DOCTOR WHO NOVELLAS

DOCTOR WHO: TIME AND RELATIVE by KIM NEWMAN

The harsh British winter of 1962/3 brings a big freeze and with it comes a new, far greater menace: terrifying icy creatures are stalking the streets, bringing death and destruction.

An adventure featuring the first Doctor and Susan.
Featuring a foreword by Justin Richards.
Deluxe edition frontispiece by Bryan Talbot.
SOLD OUT Standard h/b ISBN: 1-903889-02-2
£25 (+ £1.50 UK p&p) Deluxe h/b ISBN: 1-903889-03-0

DOCTOR WHO: CITADEL OF DREAMS by DAVE STONE

In the city-state of Hokesh, time plays tricks; the present is unreliable, the future impossible to intimate.

An adventure featuring the seventh Doctor and Ace.
Featuring a foreword by Andrew Cartmel.
Deluxe edition frontispiece by Lee Sullivan.
£10 (+ £1.50 UK p&p) Standard h/b ISBN: 1-903889-04-9
£25 (+ £1.50 UK p&p) Deluxe h/b ISBN: 1-903889-05-7

DOCTOR WHO: NIGHTDREAMERS by TOM ARDEN

Perihelion Night on the wooded moon Verd. A time of strange sightings, ghosts, and celebration. But what of the mysterious and terrifying Nightdreamers? And of the Nightdreamer King?

An adventure featuring the third Doctor and Jo.
Featuring a foreword by Katy Manning.
Deluxe edition frontispiece by Martin McKenna.
£10 (+ £1.50 UK p&p) Standard h/b ISBN: 1-903889-06-5
£25 (+ £1.50 UK p&p) Deluxe h/b ISBN: 1-903889-07-3

DOCTOR WHO: GHOST SHIP by KEITH TOPPING

The TARDIS lands in the most haunted place on Earth, the luxury ocean liner the Queen Mary on its way from Southampton to New York in the year 1963. But why do ghosts from the past, the present and, perhaps even the future, seek out the Doctor?

An adventure featuring the fourth Doctor.
Featuring a foreword by Hugh Lamb.
Deluxe edition frontispiece by Dariusz Jasiczak.
£5.99 (+ £1.50 UK p&p) p/b ISBN: 1-903889-32-4
SOLD OUT Standard h/b ISBN: 1-903889-08-1
£25 (+ £1.50 UK p&p) Deluxe h/b ISBN: 1-903889-09-X

DOCTOR WHO: FOREIGN DEVILS by ANDREW CARTMEL

The Doctor, Jamie and Zoe find themselves joining forces with a psychic investigator named Carnacki to solve a series of strange murders in an English country house.

An adventure featuring the second Doctor, Jamie and Zoe.
Featuring a foreword by Mike Ashley.
Deluxe edition frontispiece by Mike Collins.
£5.99 (+ £1.50 UK p&p) p/b ISBN: 1-903889-33-2
SOLD OUT Standard h/b ISBN: 1-903889-10-3
£25 (+ £1.50 UK p&p) Deluxe h/b ISBN: 1-903889-11-1

DOCTOR WHO: RIP TIDE by LOUISE COOPER

Strange things are afoot in a sleepy Cornish village. Strangers are hanging about the harbour and a mysterious object is retrieved from the sea bed. Then the locals start getting sick. The Doctor is perhaps the only person who can help, but can he discover the truth in time?

An adventure featuring the eighth Doctor.
Featuring a foreword by Stephen Gallagher.
Deluxe edition frontispiece by Fred Gambino.
£10 (+ £1.50 UK p&p) Standard h/b ISBN: 1-903889-12-X
£25 (+ £1.50 UK p&p) Deluxe h/b ISBN: 1-903889-13-8

DOCTOR WHO: WONDERLAND by MARK CHADBOURN

San Francisco 1967. A place of love and peace as the hippy movement is in full swing. Summer, however, has lost her boyfriend, and fears him dead, destroyed by a new type of drug nicknamed Blue Moonbeams. Her only friends are three English tourists: Ben and Polly, and the mysterious Doctor. But will any of them help Summer, and what is the strange threat posed by the Blue Moonbeams?

An adventure featuring the second Doctor, Ben and Polly.
Featuring a foreword by Graham Joyce.
Deluxe edition frontispiece by Dominic Harman.
£10 (+ £1.50 UK p&p) Standard h/b ISBN: 1-903889-14-6
£25 (+ £1.50 UK p&p) Deluxe h/b ISBN: 1-903889-15-4

DOCTOR WHO: SHELL SHOCK by SIMON A. FORWARD

The Doctor is stranded on an alien beach with only intelligent crabs and a madman for company. How can he possibly rescue Peri, who was lost at sea the same time as he and the TARDIS?

An adventure featuring the sixth Doctor and Peri.
Featuring a foreword by Guy N. Smith.
Deluxe edition frontispiece by Bob Covington.
£10 (+ £1.50 UK p&p) Standard h/b ISBN: 1-903889-16-2
£25 (+ £1.50 UK p&p) Deluxe h/b ISBN: 1-903889-17-0

DOCTOR WHO: THE CABINET OF LIGHT
by DANIEL O'MAHONY

Where is the Doctor? Everyone is hunting him. Honoré Lechasseur, a time sensitive 'fixer', is hired by mystery woman Emily Blandish to find him. But what is his connection with London in 1949? Lechasseur is about to discover that following in the Doctor's footsteps can be a difficult task.

An adventure featuring the Doctor.
Featuring a foreword by Chaz Brenchley.
Deluxe edition frontispiece by John Higgins.
£10 (+ £1.50 UK p&p) Standard h/b ISBN: 1-903889-18-9
£25 (+ £1.50 UK p&p) Deluxe h/b ISBN: 1-903889-19-7

DOCTOR WHO: FALLEN GODS
by KATE ORMAN and JONATHAN BLUM

In ancient Akrotiri, a young girl is learning the mysteries of magic from a tutor, who, quite literally, fell from the skies. With his encouragement she can surf the timestreams and see something of the future. But then the demons come.

An adventure featuring the eighth Doctor
Featuring a foreword by Storm Constantine.
Deluxe edition frontispiece by Daryl Joyce.
£10 (+ £1.50 UK p&p) Standard h/b ISBN: 1-903889-20-1
£25 (+ £1.50 UK p&p) Deluxe h/b ISBN: 1-903889-21-9

DOCTOR WHO: FRAYED by TARA SAMMS

On a blasted world, the Doctor and Susan find themselves in the middle of a war they cannot understand. With Susan missing and the Doctor captured, who will save the people from the enemies both from outside and within?

An adventure featuring the first Doctor and Susan.
Featuring a foreword by Stephen Laws.
Deluxe edition frontispiece by Chris Moore.
£10 (+ £1.50 UK p&p) Standard h/b ISBN: 1-903889-22-7
£25 (+ £1.50 UK p&p) Deluxe h/b ISBN: 1-903889-23-5

DOCTOR WHO: EYE OF THE TYGER by PAUL MCAULEY

On a spaceship trapped in the orbit of a black hole, the Doctor finds himself fighting to save a civilisation from extinction.

An adventure featuring the eighth Doctor.
Featuring a foreword by Neil Gaiman.
Deluxe edition frontispiece by Jim Burns.
£10 (+ £1.50 UK p&p) Standard h/b ISBN: 1-903889-24-3
£25 (+ £1.50 UK p&p) Deluxe h/b ISBN: 1-903889-25-1
Published November 2003